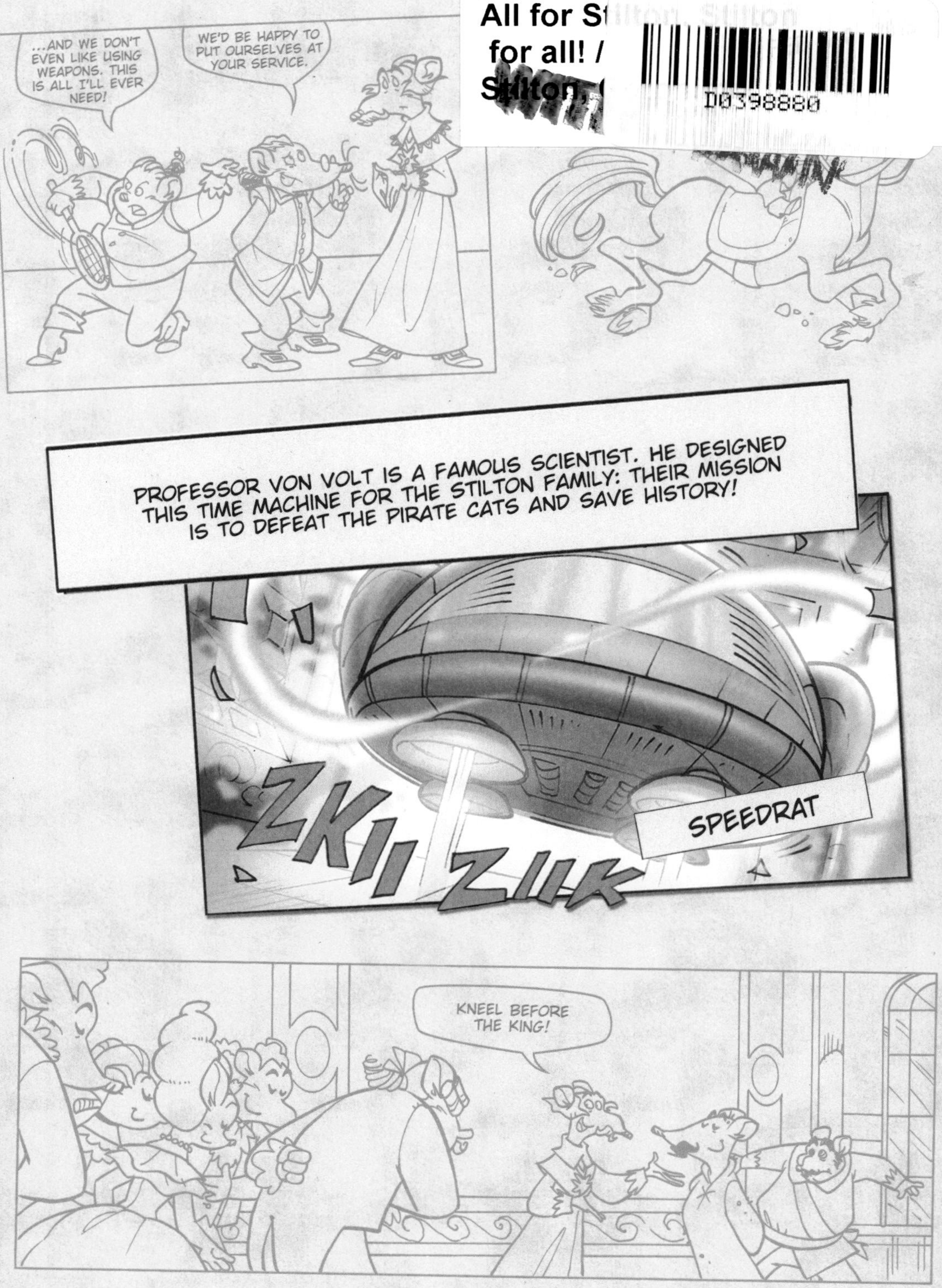
...AND WE DON'T EVEN LIKE USING WEAPONS. THIS IS ALL I'LL EVER NEED!
WE'D BE HAPPY TO PUT OURSELVES AT YOUR SERVICE.
PROFESSOR VON VOLT IS A FAMOUS SCIENTIST. HE DESIGNED THIS TIME MACHINE FOR THE STILTON FAMILY: THEIR MISSION IS TO DEFEAT THE PIRATE CATS AND SAVE HISTORY!
ZKII ZIIK
SPEEDRAT
KNEEL BEFORE THE KING!

Geronimo Stilton

PAPERCUTZ™

Geronimo Stilton & Thea Stilton

GRAPHIC NOVELS AVAILABLE FROM PAPERCUTZ™

...ALSO AVAILABLE WHEREVER E-BOOKS ARE SOLD!

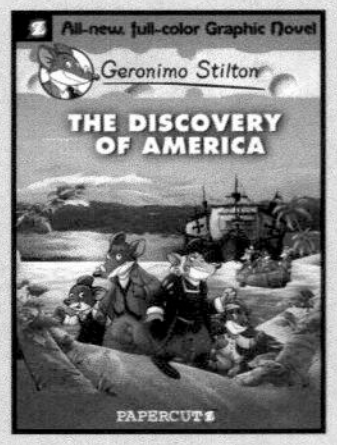
All-new, full-color Graphic Novel
Geronimo Stilton
THE DISCOVERY OF AMERICA
PAPERCUTZ

#1 "The Discovery of America"

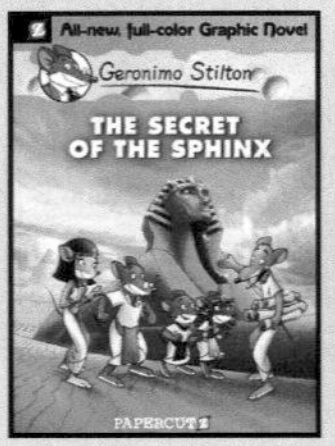
All-new, full-color Graphic Novel
Geronimo Stilton
THE SECRET OF THE SPHINX
PAPERCUTZ

#2 "The Secret of the Sphinx"

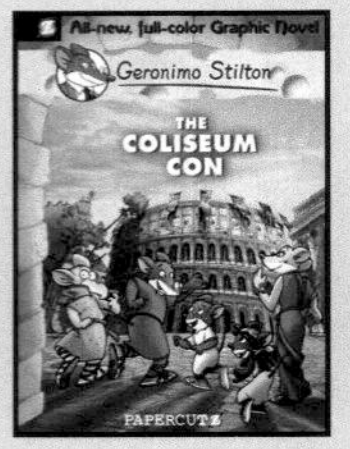
All-new, full-color Graphic Novel
Geronimo Stilton
THE COLISEUM CON
PAPERCUTZ

#3 "The Coliseum Con"

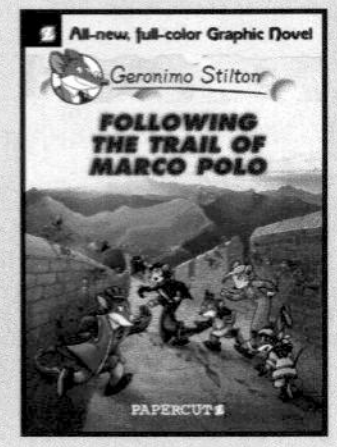
All-new, full-color Graphic Novel
Geronimo Stilton
FOLLOWING THE TRAIL OF MARCO POLO
PAPERCUTZ

#4 "Following the Trail of Marco Polo"

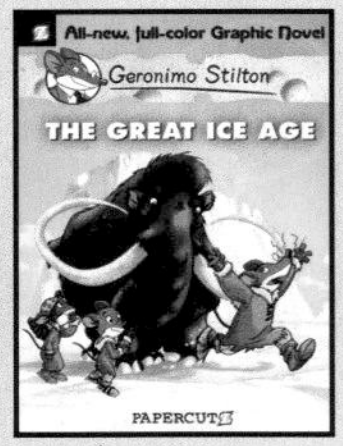
All-new, full-color Graphic Novel
Geronimo Stilton
THE GREAT ICE AGE
PAPERCUTZ

#5 "The Great Ice Age"

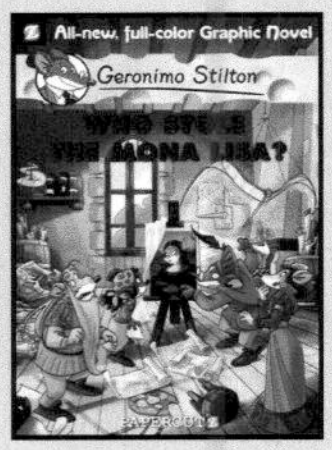
All-new, full-color Graphic Novel
Geronimo Stilton
PAPERCUTZ

#6 "Who Stole The Mona Lisa?"

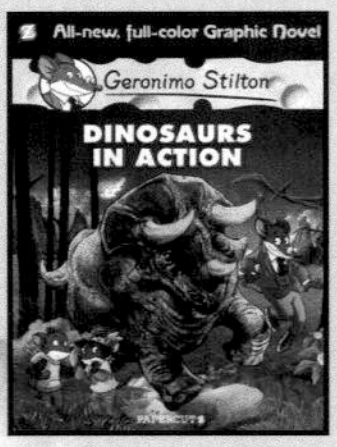
All-new, full-color Graphic Novel
Geronimo Stilton
DINOSAURS IN ACTION
PAPERCUTZ

#7 "Dinosaurs in Action"

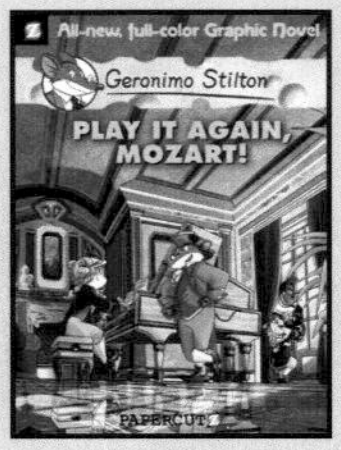
All-new, full-color Graphic Novel
Geronimo Stilton
PLAY IT AGAIN, MOZART!
PAPERCUTZ

#8 "Play It Again, Mozart!"

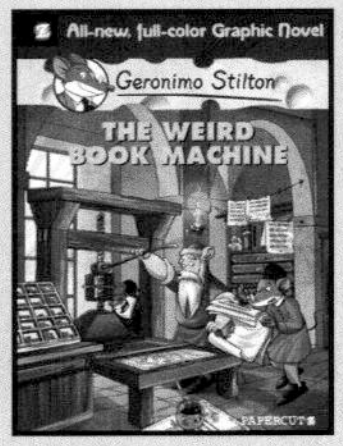
All-new, full-color Graphic Novel
Geronimo Stilton
THE WEIRD BOOK MACHINE
PAPERCUTZ

#9 "The Weird Book Machine"

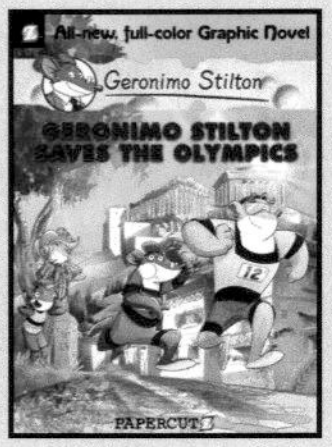
All-new, full-color Graphic Novel
Geronimo Stilton
GERONIMO STILTON SAVES THE OLYMPICS
PAPERCUTZ

#10 "Geronimo Stilton Saves the Olympics"

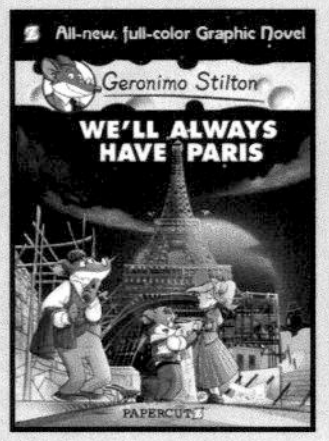
All-new, full-color Graphic Novel
Geronimo Stilton
WE'LL ALWAYS HAVE PARIS
PAPERCUTZ

#11 "We'll Always Have Paris"

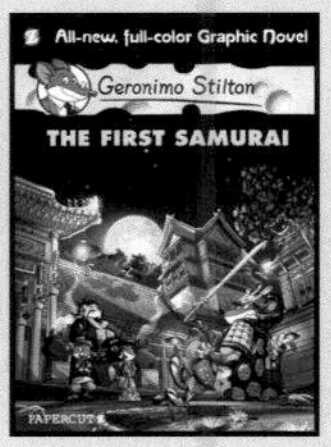
All-new, full-color Graphic Novel
Geronimo Stilton
THE FIRST SAMURAI
PAPERCUTZ

#12 "The First Samurai"

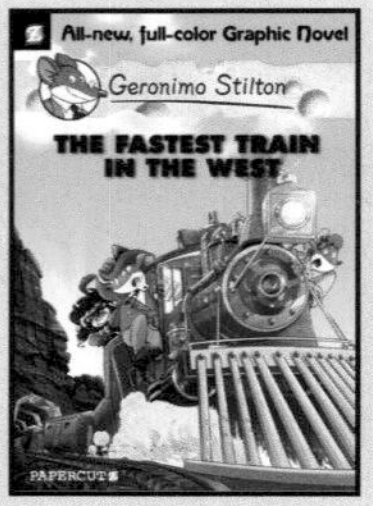
All-new, full-color Graphic Novel
Geronimo Stilton
THE FASTEST TRAIN IN THE WEST
PAPERCUTZ

#13 "The Fastest Train in the West"

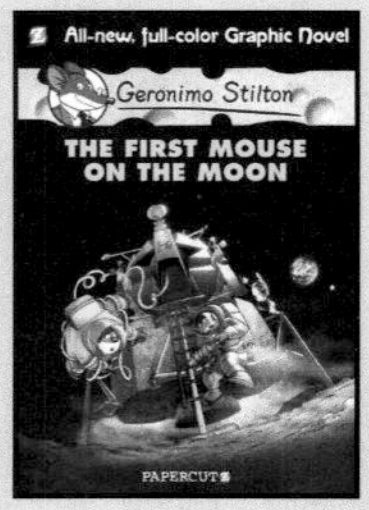
All-new, full-color Graphic Novel
Geronimo Stilton
THE FIRST MOUSE ON THE MOON
PAPERCUTZ

#14 "The First Mouse on the Moon"

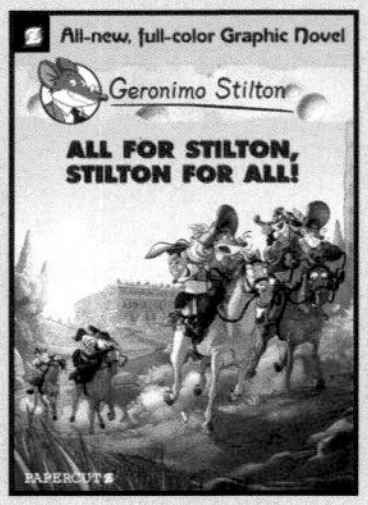
All-new, full-color Graphic Novel
Geronimo Stilton
ALL FOR STILTON, STILTON FOR ALL!
PAPERCUTZ

#15 "All for Stilton, Stilton for All!"

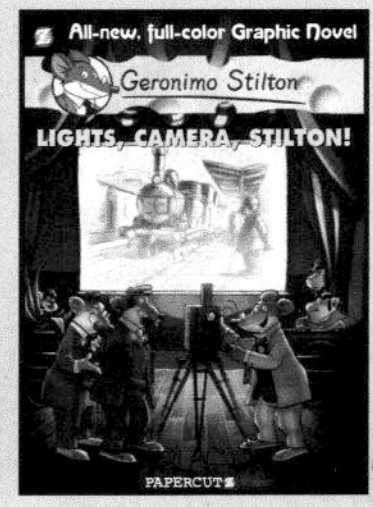
All-new, full-color Graphic Novel
Geronimo Stilton
LIGHTS, CAMERA, STILTON!
PAPERCUTZ

#16 "Lights, Camera, Stilton!"

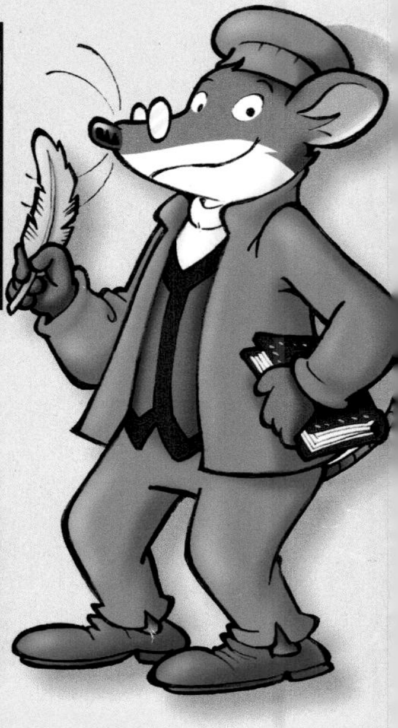

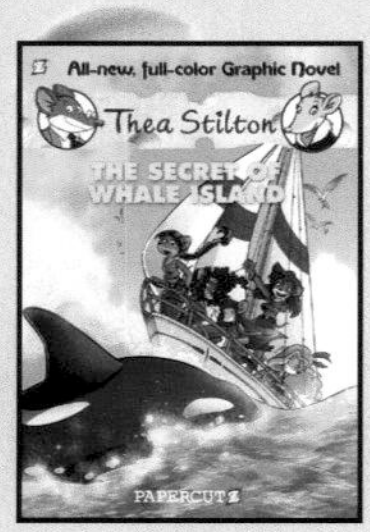
All-new, full-color Graphic Novel
Thea Stilton
THE SECRET OF WHALE ISLAND
PAPERCUTZ

#1 "The Secret of Whale Island"

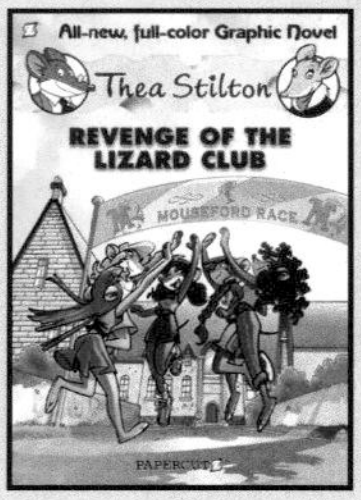
All-new, full-color Graphic Novel
Thea Stilton
REVENGE OF THE LIZARD CLUB
MOUSEFORD RACE
PAPERCUTZ

#2 "Revenge of the Lizard Club"

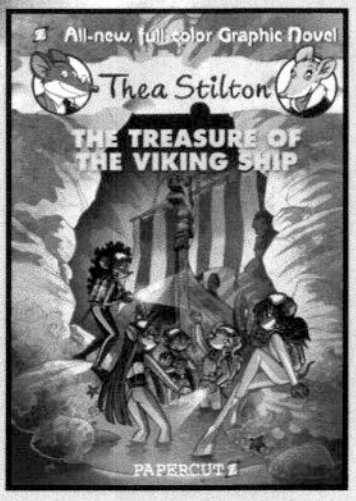
All-new, full-color Graphic Novel
Thea Stilton
THE TREASURE OF THE VIKING SHIP
PAPERCUTZ

#3 "The Treasure of the Viking Ship"

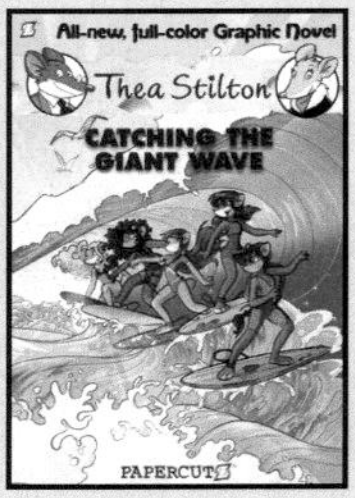
All-new, full-color Graphic Novel
Thea Stilton
CATCHING THE GIANT WAVE
PAPERCUTZ

#4 "Catching the Giant Wave"

papercutz.com

GERONIMO STILTON and THEA STILTON graphic novels are available for $9.99 each only in hardcover. Available from booksellers everywhere. You can also order online from papercutz.com. Or call 1-800-886-1223, Monday through Friday, 9 – 5 EST. MC, Visa, and AmEx accepted. To order by mail, please add $4.00 for postage and handling for first book ordered, $1.00 for each additional book and make check payable to NBM Publishing.
Send to: Papercutz, 160 Broadway, Suite 700, East Wing, New York, NY 10038.

Geronimo Stilton

ALL FOR STILTON, STILTON FOR ALL!
By Geronimo Stilton

PAPERCUTZ
NEW YORK

ALL FOR STILTON, STILTON FOR ALL!
© 2014 EDIZIONI PIEMME S.p.A.
Corso Como 15, 20145,
Milan, Italy
Graphics and Illustrations © Atlantyca Entertainment S.p.A. 2014
Geronimo Stilton names, characters, and related indicia are copyright, trademark, and exclusive
license of Atlantyca S.p.A.
All rights reserved.
The moral right of the author has been asserted.

Text by Geronimo Stilton
Story by Michele Foschini and Leonardo Favia
Script by Leonardo Favia
Illustrations by Federica Salfo
Color by Mirka Andolfo
Cover by Ennio Bufi and Mirka Andolfo
Based on an original idea by Elisabetta Dami

© 2014 – for this work in English language by Papercutz.
International Rights © Atlantyca S.p.A Via Leopardi 8-20123 Milan, Italy
Original title: "Uno per tutti, tutti per Stilton!"

www.geronimostilton.com

Stilton is the name of a famous English cheese. It is a registered trademark of the Stilton Cheese
Makers' Association. For more information go to www.stiltoncheese.com

No part of this book may be stored, reproduced, or transmitted in any form or by any means,
electronic or mechanical, including photocopying, recording, or by any information storage and
retrieval system, without written permission from the copyright holder.
FOR INFORMATION PLEASE ADDRESS ATLANTYCA S.p.A.
Via Leopardi 8 20123 Milan Italy –foreignrights@atlantyca.it - www.atlantyca.com

Nanette McGuinness – Translation
Big Bird Satryb – Lettering & Production
Beth Scorzato, Jeff Whitman – Production Coordinators
Robyn Chapman – Editor
Michael Petranek – Associate Editor
Jim Salicrup
Editor-in-Chief

ISBN: 978-1-62991-149-6

Printed in China.
December 2014 by WKT Co. LTD.
3/F Phase 1 Leader Industrial Centre
188 Texaco Road, Tsuen Wan, N.T.
Hong Kong

Papercutz books may be purchased for business or promotional use. For information on bulk purchases
please contact Macmillan Corporate and Premium Sales Department at (800) 221-7945 x5442.

Distributed by Macmillan
First Papercutz Printing

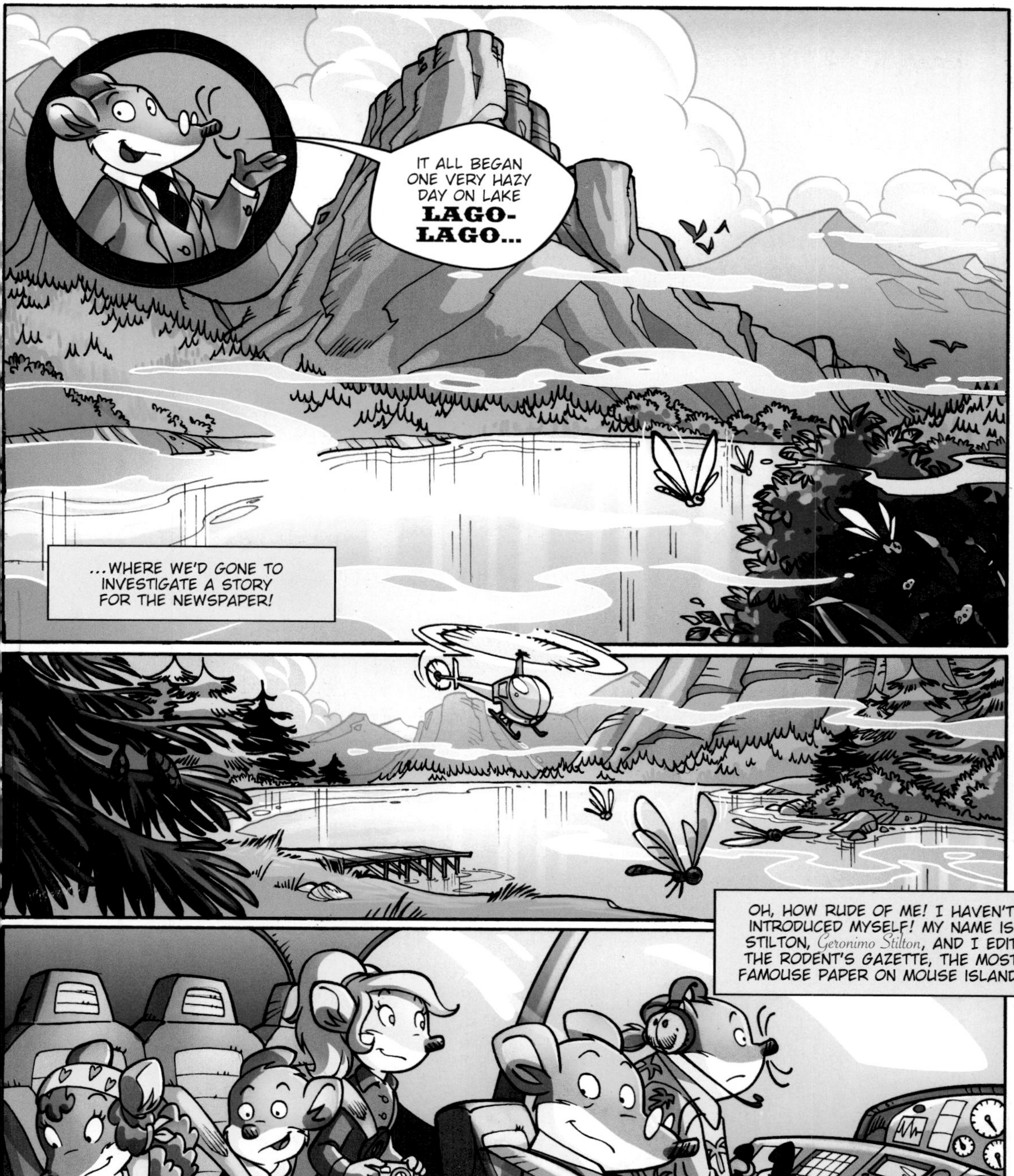
IT ALL BEGAN ONE VERY HAZY DAY ON LAKE **LAGO-LAGO...**
...WHERE WE'D GONE TO INVESTIGATE A STORY FOR THE NEWSPAPER!
OH, HOW RUDE OF ME! I HAVEN'T INTRODUCED MYSELF! MY NAME IS STILTON, *Geronimo Stilton*, AND I EDIT THE RODENT'S GAZETTE, THE MOST FAMOUSE PAPER ON MOUSE ISLAND!

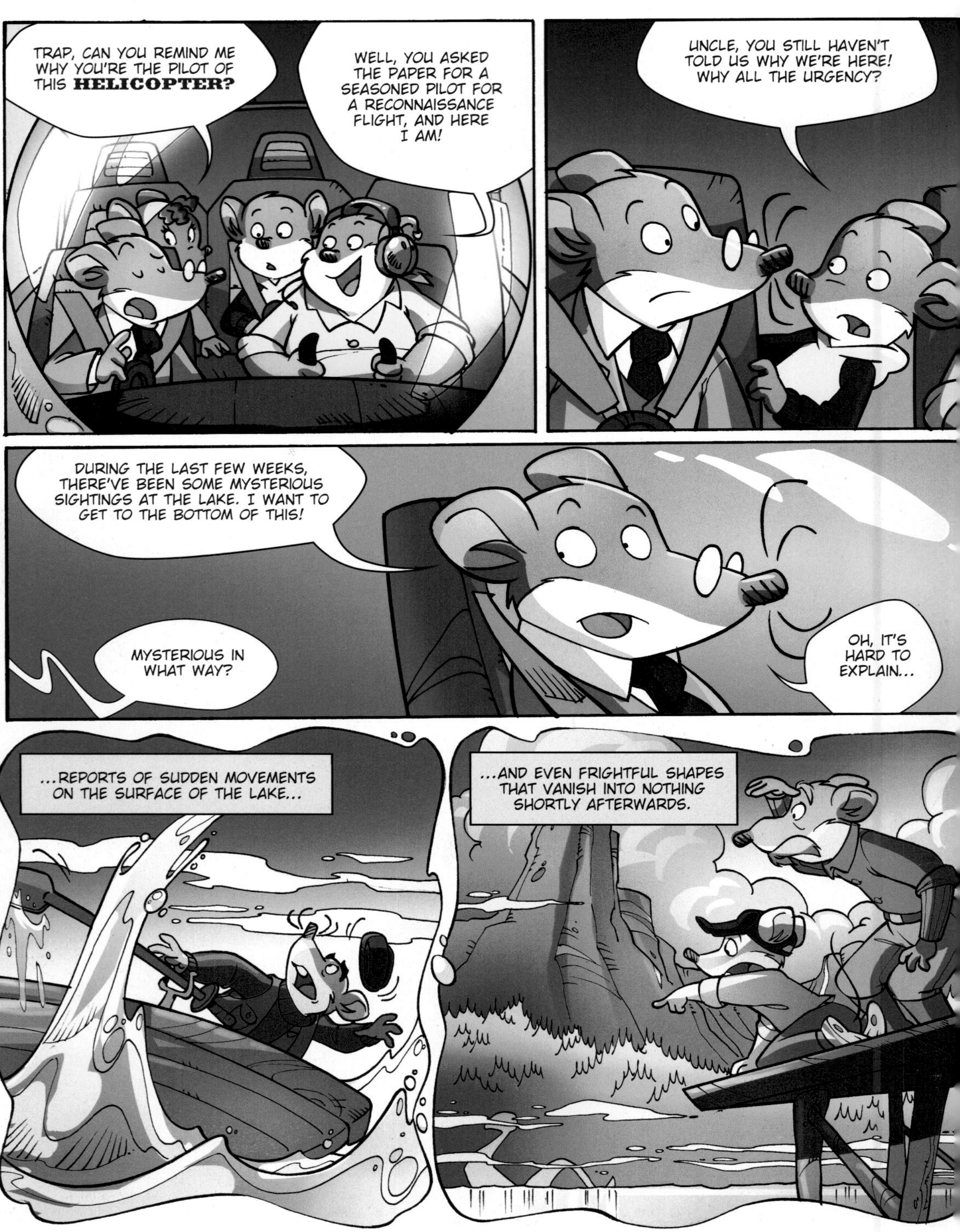
TRAP, CAN YOU REMIND ME WHY YOU'RE THE PILOT OF THIS **HELICOPTER?**
WELL, YOU ASKED THE PAPER FOR A SEASONED PILOT FOR A RECONNAISSANCE FLIGHT, AND HERE I AM!
UNCLE, YOU STILL HAVEN'T TOLD US WHY WE'RE HERE! WHY ALL THE URGENCY?
DURING THE LAST FEW WEEKS, THERE'VE BEEN SOME MYSTERIOUS SIGHTINGS AT THE LAKE. I WANT TO GET TO THE BOTTOM OF THIS!
MYSTERIOUS IN WHAT WAY?
OH, IT'S HARD TO EXPLAIN...
...REPORTS OF SUDDEN MOVEMENTS ON THE SURFACE OF THE LAKE...
...AND EVEN FRIGHTFUL SHAPES THAT VANISH INTO NOTHING SHORTLY AFTERWARDS.

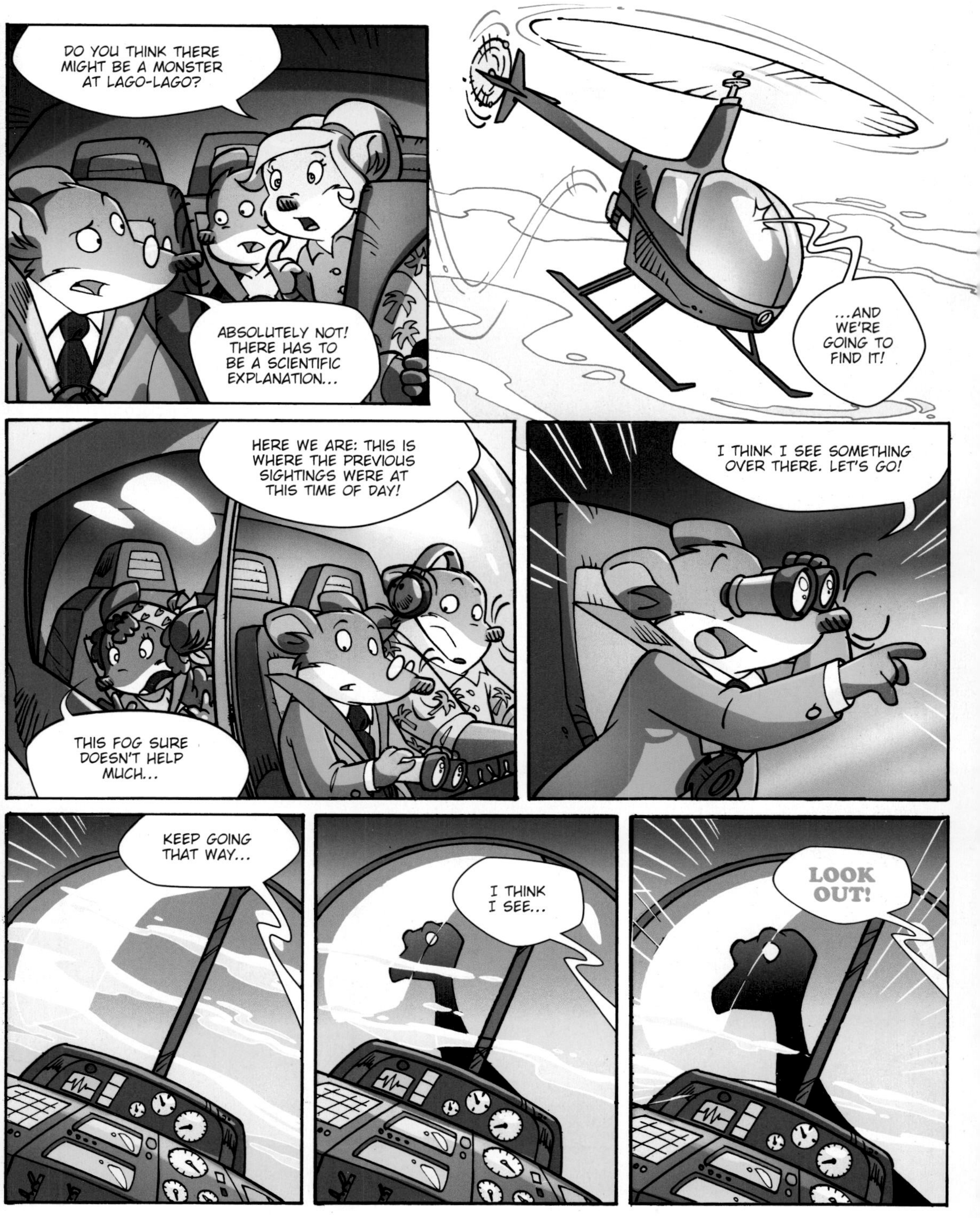
DO YOU THINK THERE MIGHT BE A MONSTER AT LAGO-LAGO?
ABSOLUTELY NOT! THERE HAS TO BE A SCIENTIFIC EXPLANATION...
...AND WE'RE GOING TO FIND IT!
HERE WE ARE: THIS IS WHERE THE PREVIOUS SIGHTINGS WERE AT THIS TIME OF DAY!
THIS FOG SURE DOESN'T HELP MUCH...
I THINK I SEE SOMETHING OVER THERE. LET'S GO!
KEEP GOING THAT WAY...
I THINK I SEE...
LOOK OUT!

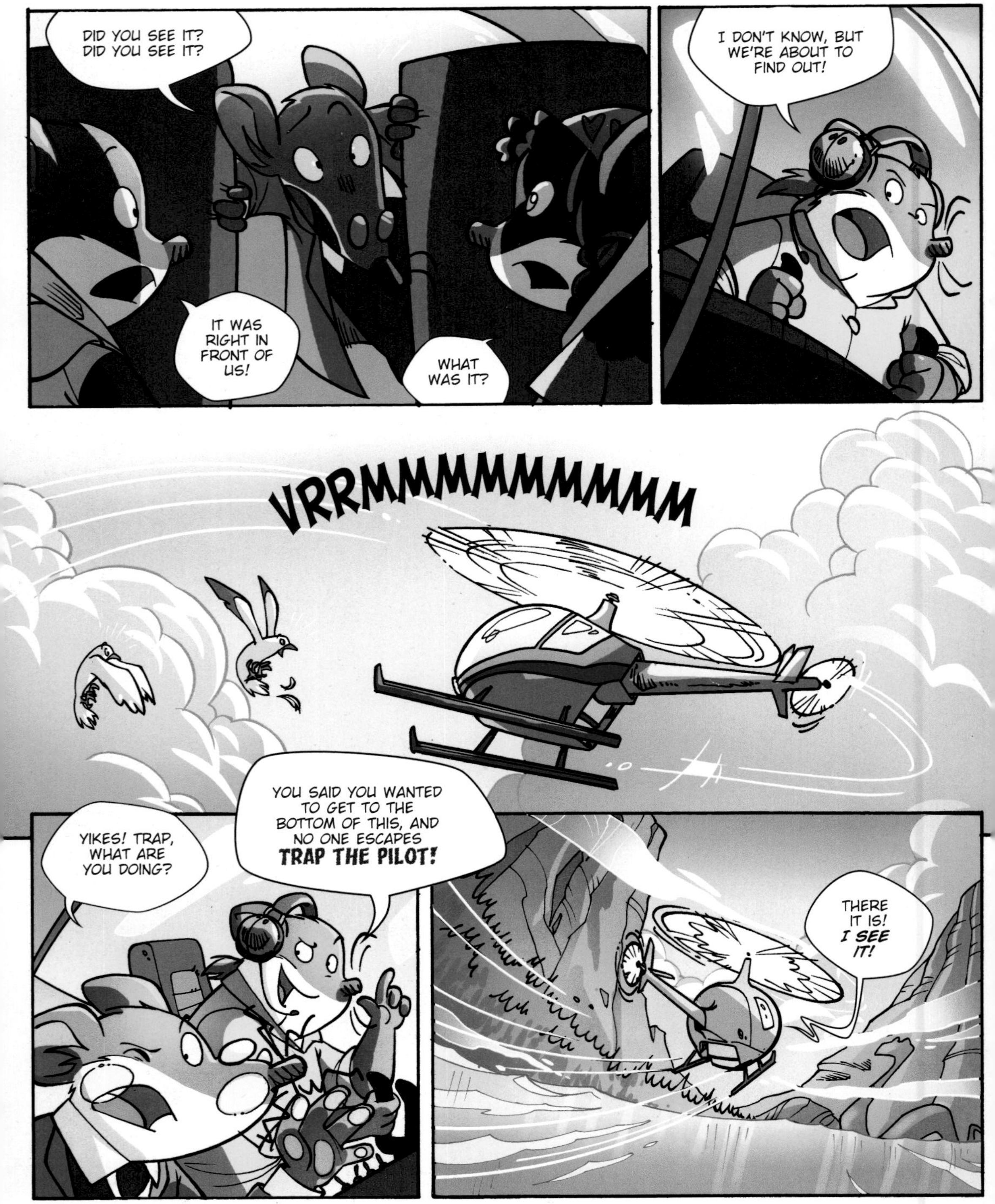
DID YOU SEE IT? DID YOU SEE IT?
IT WAS RIGHT IN FRONT OF US!
WHAT WAS IT?
I DON'T KNOW, BUT WE'RE ABOUT TO FIND OUT!
VRRMMMMMMMMMM
YIKES! TRAP, WHAT ARE YOU DOING?
YOU SAID YOU WANTED TO GET TO THE BOTTOM OF THIS, AND NO ONE ESCAPES TRAP THE PILOT!
THERE IT IS! I SEE IT!

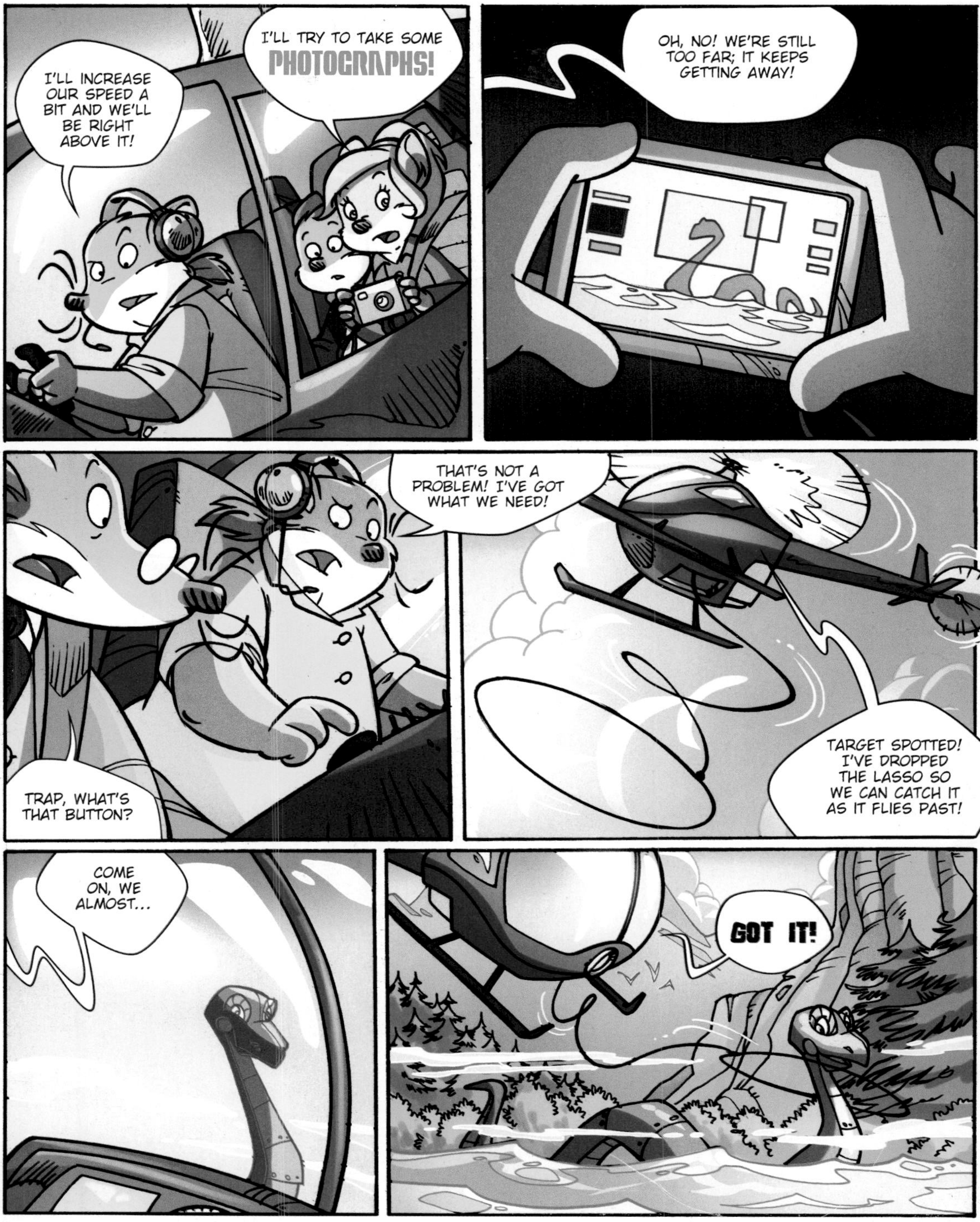
I'LL INCREASE OUR SPEED A BIT AND WE'LL BE RIGHT ABOVE IT!
I'LL TRY TO TAKE SOME PHOTOGRAPHS!
OH, NO! WE'RE STILL TOO FAR; IT KEEPS GETTING AWAY!
TRAP, WHAT'S THAT BUTTON?
THAT'S NOT A PROBLEM! I'VE GOT WHAT WE NEED!
TARGET SPOTTED! I'VE DROPPED THE LASSO SO WE CAN CATCH IT AS IT FLIES PAST!
COME ON, WE ALMOST...
GOT IT!

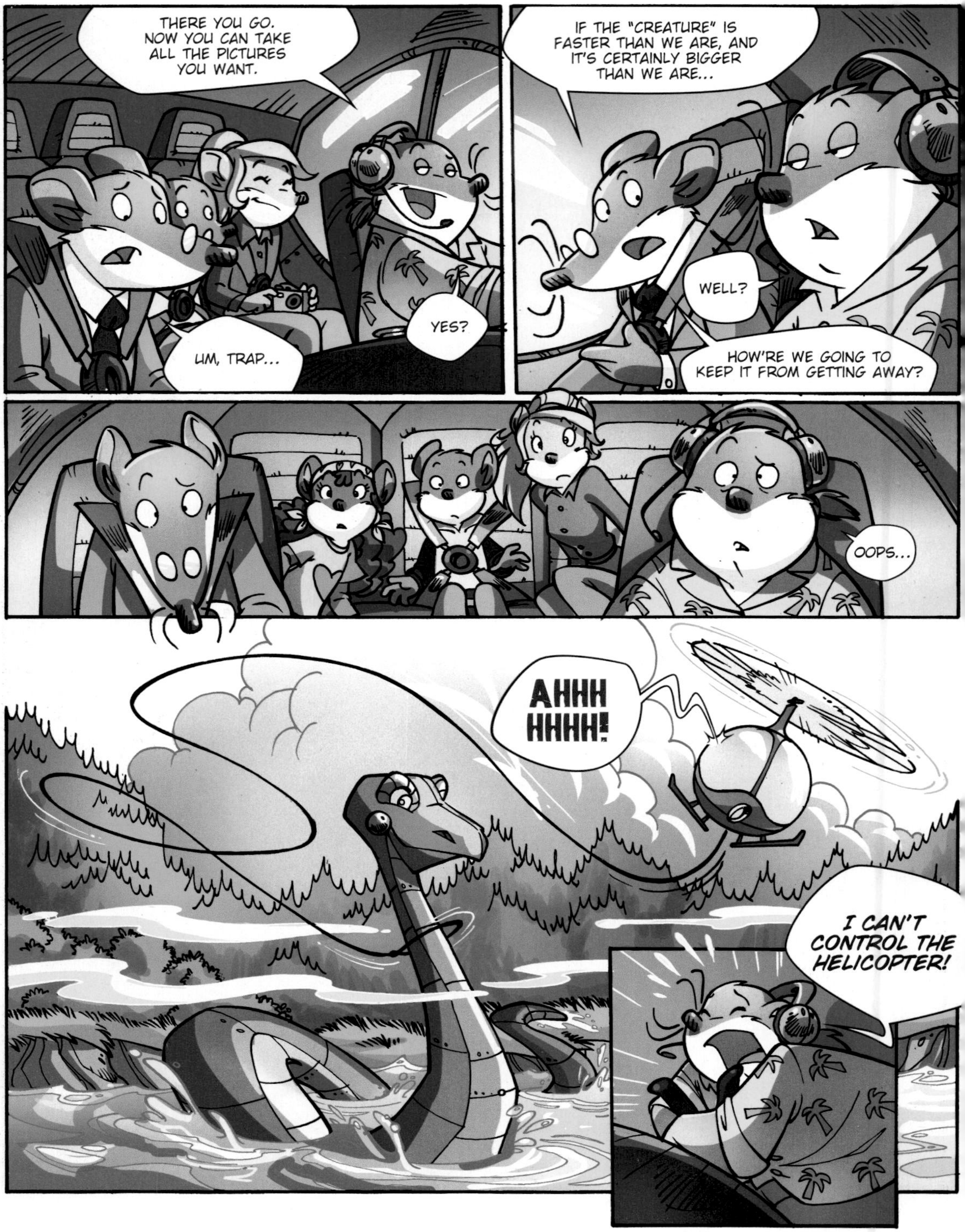
THERE YOU GO. NOW YOU CAN TAKE ALL THE PICTURES YOU WANT.
UM, TRAP...
YES?
IF THE "CREATURE" IS FASTER THAN WE ARE, AND IT'S CERTAINLY BIGGER THAN WE ARE...
WELL?
HOW'RE WE GOING TO KEEP IT FROM GETTING AWAY?
OOPS...
AHHH HHHH!
I CAN'T CONTROL THE HELICOPTER!

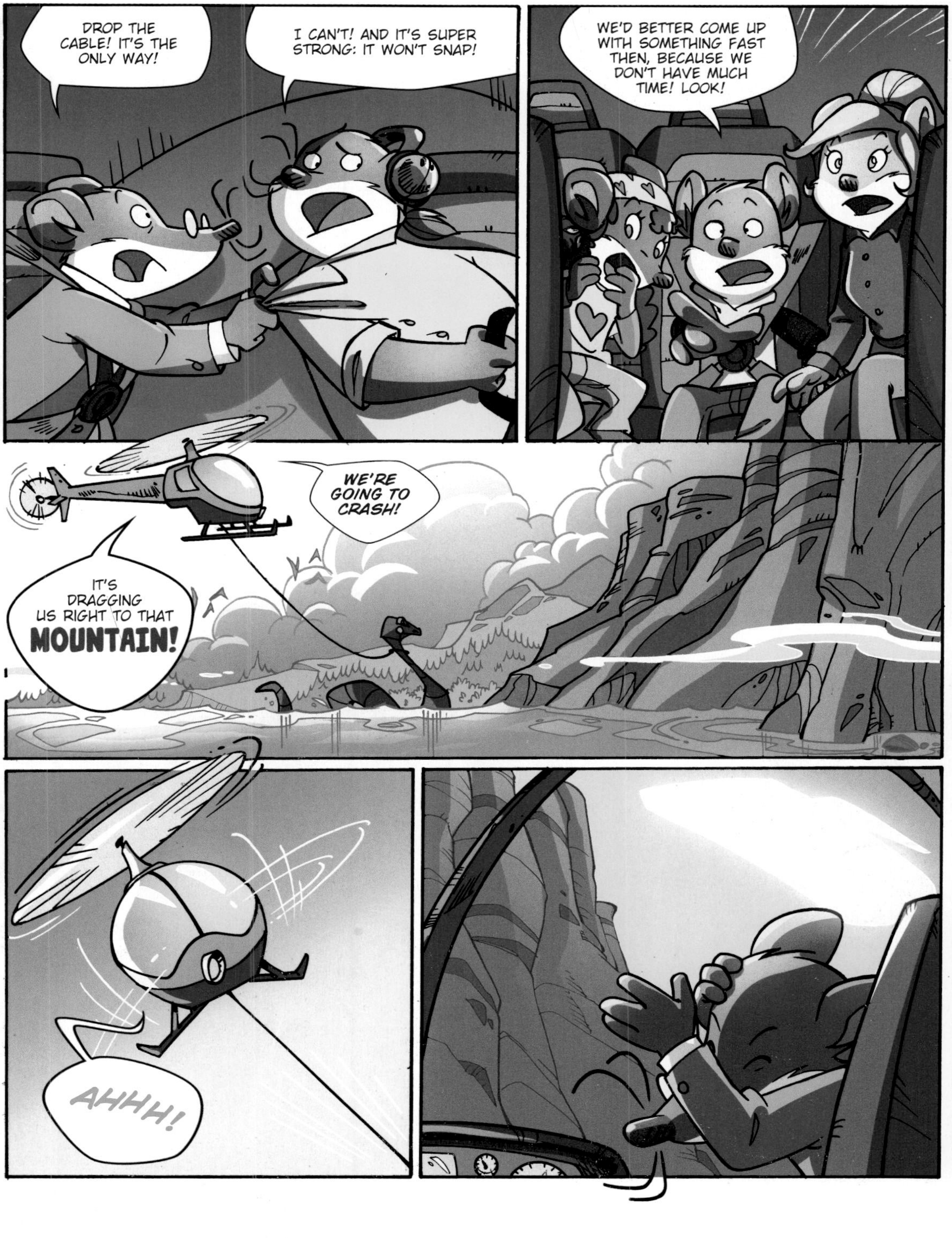
DROP THE CABLE! IT'S THE ONLY WAY!
I CAN'T! AND IT'S SUPER STRONG: IT WON'T SNAP!
WE'D BETTER COME UP WITH SOMETHING FAST THEN, BECAUSE WE DON'T HAVE MUCH TIME! LOOK!
WE'RE GOING TO CRASH!
IT'S DRAGGING US RIGHT TO THAT MOUNTAIN!
AHHH!

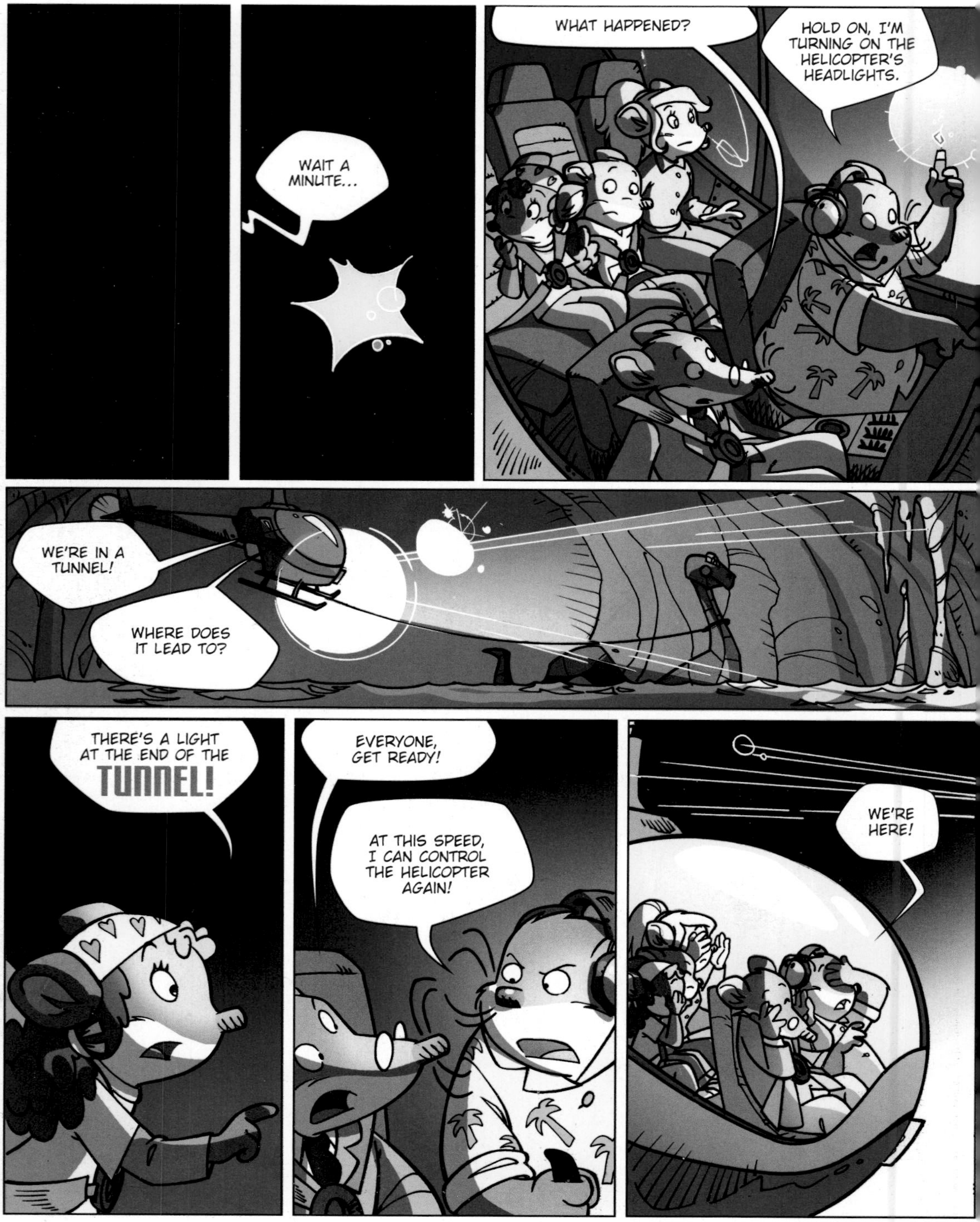
WAIT A MINUTE...
WHAT HAPPENED?
HOLD ON, I'M TURNING ON THE HELICOPTER'S HEADLIGHTS.
WE'RE IN A TUNNEL!
WHERE DOES IT LEAD TO?
THERE'S A LIGHT AT THE END OF THE TUNNEL!
EVERYONE, GET READY!
AT THIS SPEED, I CAN CONTROL THE HELICOPTER AGAIN!
WE'RE HERE!

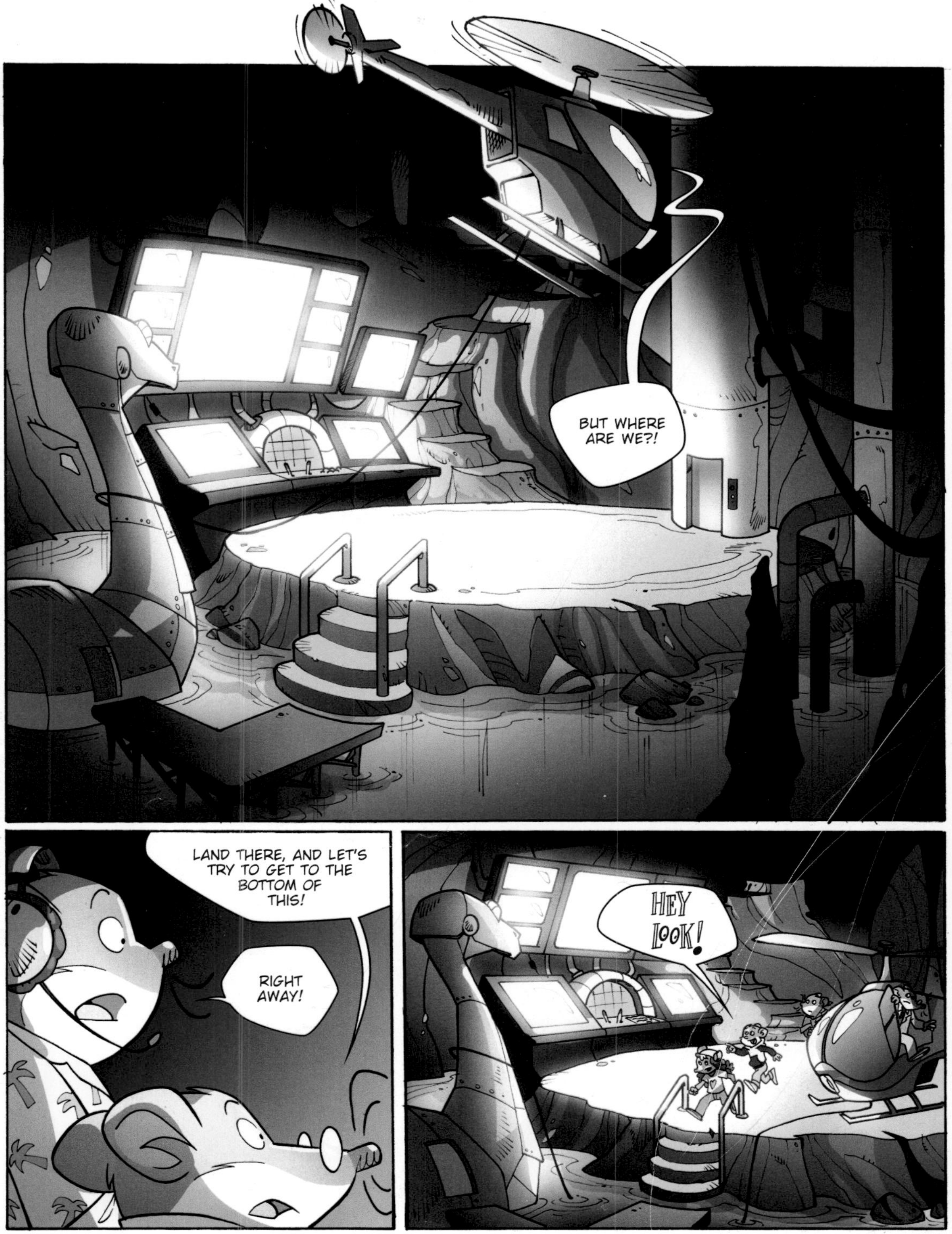
BUT WHERE ARE WE?!
LAND THERE, AND LET'S TRY TO GET TO THE BOTTOM OF THIS!
RIGHT AWAY!
HEY LOOK!

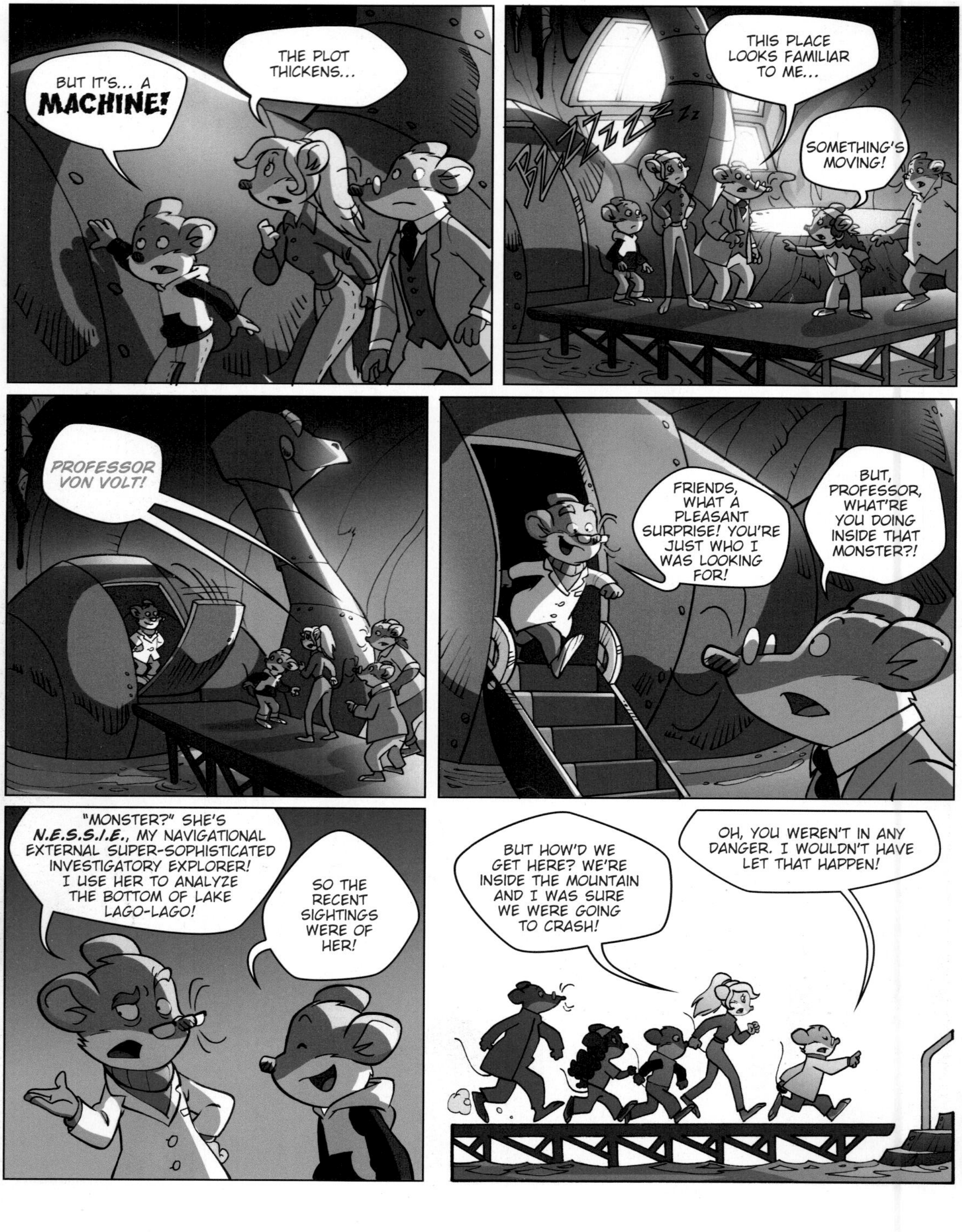
BUT IT'S... A MACHINE!
THE PLOT THICKENS...
THIS PLACE LOOKS FAMILIAR TO ME...
BZZZZZZZZ
SOMETHING'S MOVING!
PROFESSOR VON VOLT!
FRIENDS, WHAT A PLEASANT SURPRISE! YOU'RE JUST WHO I WAS LOOKING FOR!
BUT, PROFESSOR, WHAT'RE YOU DOING INSIDE THAT MONSTER?!
"MONSTER?" SHE'S N.E.S.S.I.E., MY NAVIGATIONAL EXTERNAL SUPER-SOPHISTICATED INVESTIGATORY EXPLORER! I USE HER TO ANALYZE THE BOTTOM OF LAKE LAGO-LAGO!
SO THE RECENT SIGHTINGS WERE OF HER!
BUT HOW'D WE GET HERE? WE'RE INSIDE THE MOUNTAIN AND I WAS SURE WE WERE GOING TO CRASH!
OH, YOU WEREN'T IN ANY DANGER. I WOULDN'T HAVE LET THAT HAPPEN!

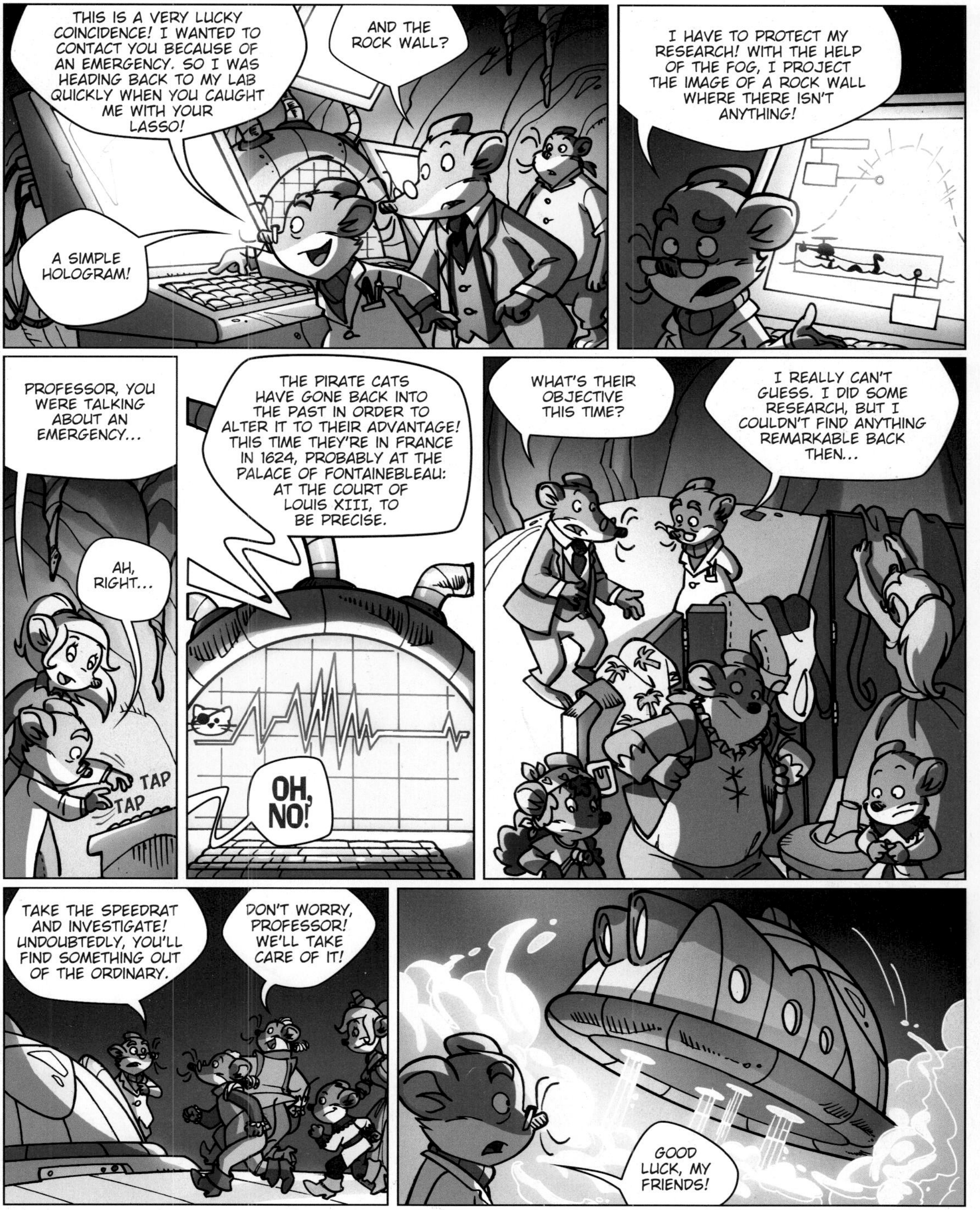
THIS IS A VERY LUCKY COINCIDENCE! I WANTED TO CONTACT YOU BECAUSE OF AN EMERGENCY. SO I WAS HEADING BACK TO MY LAB QUICKLY WHEN YOU CAUGHT ME WITH YOUR LASSO!
AND THE ROCK WALL?
A SIMPLE HOLOGRAM!
I HAVE TO PROTECT MY RESEARCH! WITH THE HELP OF THE FOG, I PROJECT THE IMAGE OF A ROCK WALL WHERE THERE ISN'T ANYTHING!
PROFESSOR, YOU WERE TALKING ABOUT AN EMERGENCY...
AH, RIGHT...
TAP
TAP
THE PIRATE CATS HAVE GONE BACK INTO THE PAST IN ORDER TO ALTER IT TO THEIR ADVANTAGE! THIS TIME THEY'RE IN FRANCE IN 1624, PROBABLY AT THE PALACE OF FONTAINEBLEAU: AT THE COURT OF LOUIS XIII, TO BE PRECISE.
OH, NO!
WHAT'S THEIR OBJECTIVE THIS TIME?
I REALLY CAN'T GUESS. I DID SOME RESEARCH, BUT I COULDN'T FIND ANYTHING REMARKABLE BACK THEN...
TAKE THE SPEEDRAT AND INVESTIGATE! UNDOUBTEDLY, YOU'LL FIND SOMETHING OUT OF THE ORDINARY.
DON'T WORRY, PROFESSOR! WE'LL TAKE CARE OF IT!
GOOD LUCK, MY FRIENDS!

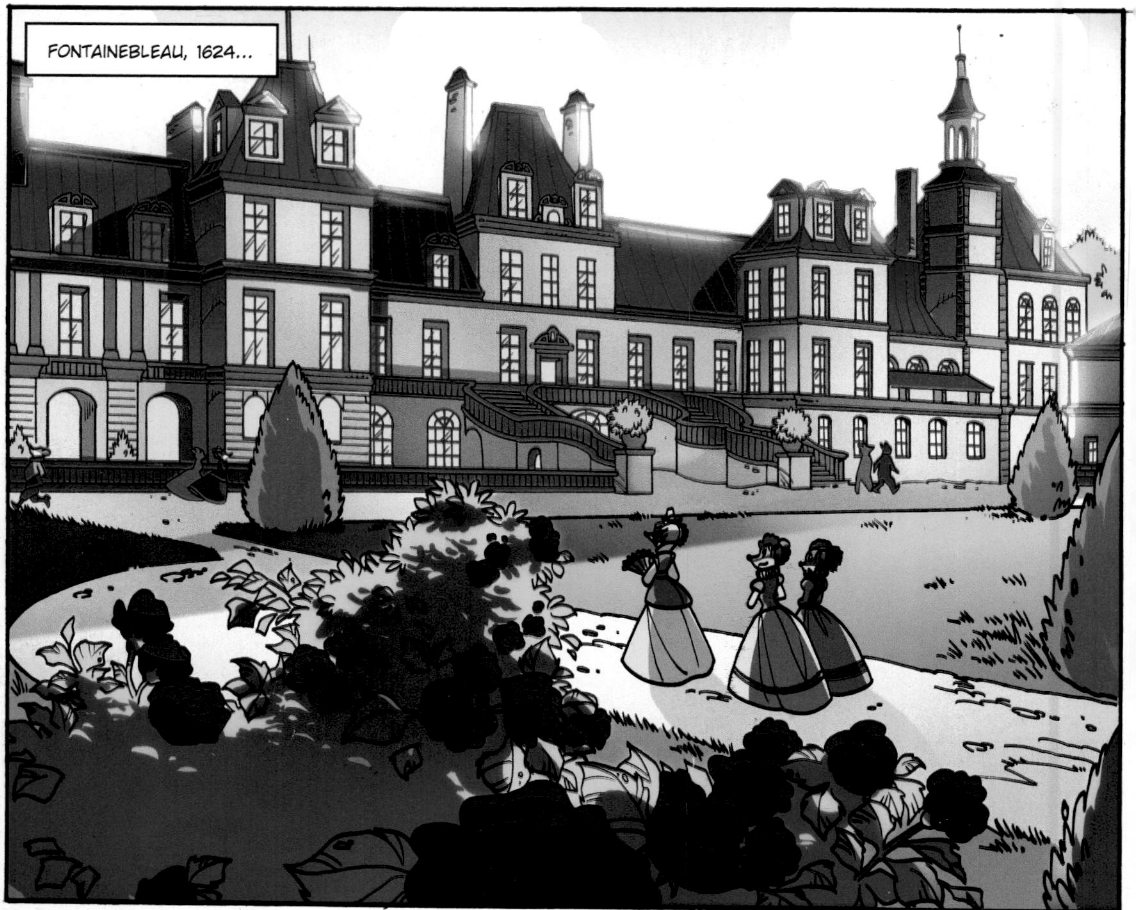
FONTAINEBLEAU, 1624...

THE PALACE OF FONTAINEBLEAU IS A CASTLE LOCATED IN THE SMALL TOWN OF THE SAME NAME-- AS OPPOSED TO THE OTHER FAMOUS FRENCH CASTLE, VERSAILLES. MANY FRENCH MONARCHS CONTRIBUTED TO THE CASTLE, STARTING WITH KING LOUIS VII IN THE 12TH CENTURY. DURING THE RENAISSANCE IT WAS REBUILT BY FRANCIS I. IT FELL OUT OF USE DURING THE FRENCH REVOLUTION, BUT WAS BROUGHT BACK BY NAPOLEON. THE CASTLE IS NOW A UNESCO WORLD HERITAGE SITE AND HOUSES A SCHOOL OF ART, ARCHITECTURE, AND MUSIC.

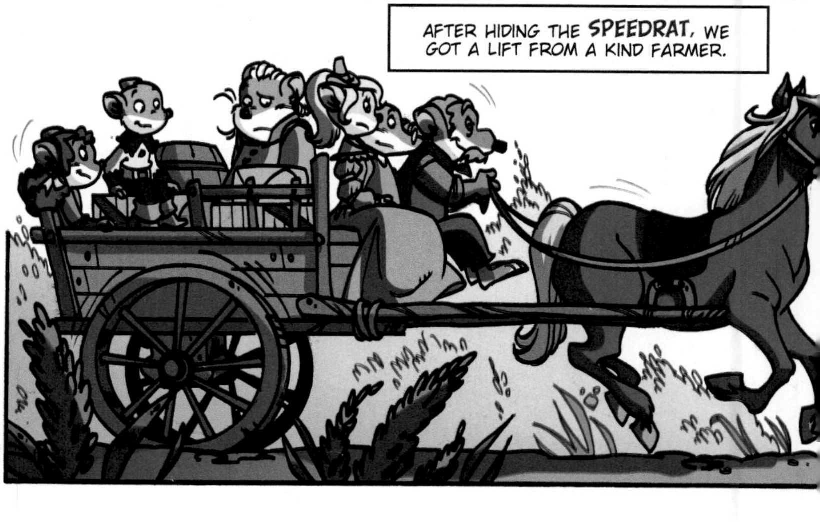
AFTER HIDING THE SPEEDRAT, WE GOT A LIFT FROM A KIND FARMER.

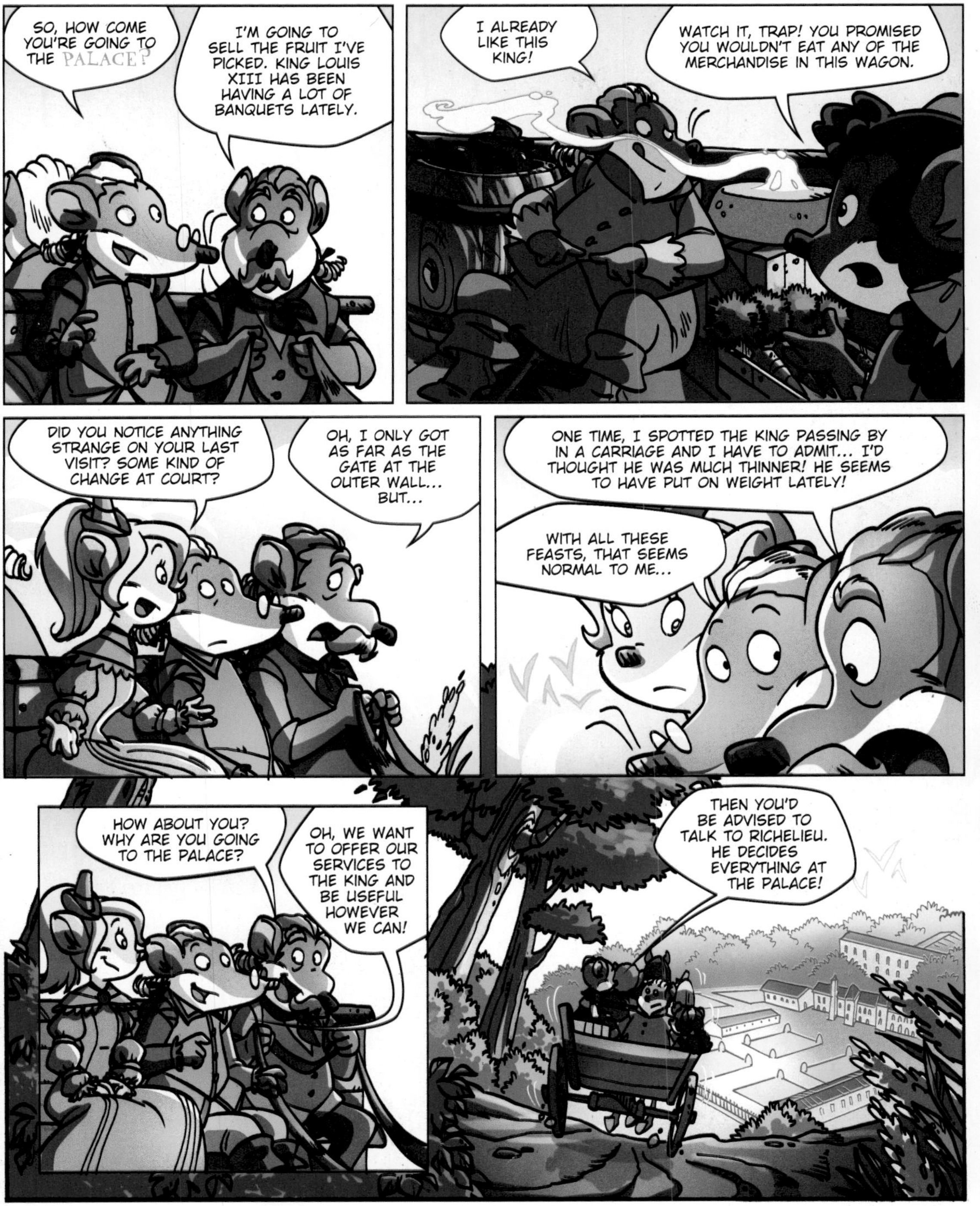
SO, HOW COME YOU'RE GOING TO THE PALACE?
I'M GOING TO SELL THE FRUIT I'VE PICKED. KING LOUIS XIII HAS BEEN HAVING A LOT OF BANQUETS LATELY.
I ALREADY LIKE THIS KING!
WATCH IT, TRAP! YOU PROMISED YOU WOULDN'T EAT ANY OF THE MERCHANDISE IN THIS WAGON.
DID YOU NOTICE ANYTHING STRANGE ON YOUR LAST VISIT? SOME KIND OF CHANGE AT COURT?
OH, I ONLY GOT AS FAR AS THE GATE AT THE OUTER WALL... BUT...
ONE TIME, I SPOTTED THE KING PASSING BY IN A CARRIAGE AND I HAVE TO ADMIT... I'D THOUGHT HE WAS MUCH THINNER! HE SEEMS TO HAVE PUT ON WEIGHT LATELY!
WITH ALL THESE FEASTS, THAT SEEMS NORMAL TO ME...
HOW ABOUT YOU? WHY ARE YOU GOING TO THE PALACE?
OH, WE WANT TO OFFER OUR SERVICES TO THE KING AND BE USEFUL HOWEVER WE CAN!
THEN YOU'D BE ADVISED TO TALK TO RICHELIEU. HE DECIDES EVERYTHING AT THE PALACE!

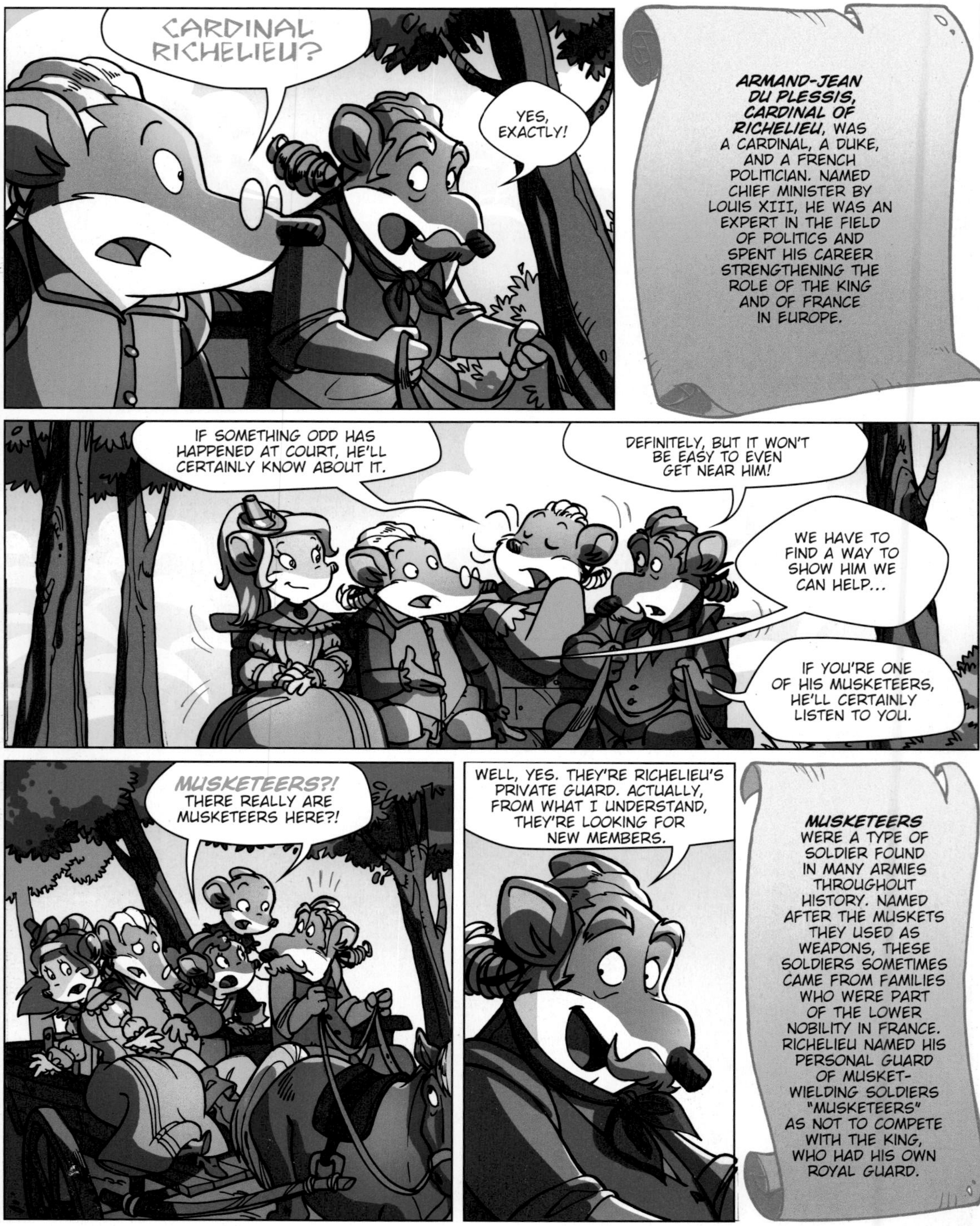
CARDINAL RICHELIEU?
YES, EXACTLY!
ARMAND-JEAN DU PLESSIS, CARDINAL OF RICHELIEU, WAS A CARDINAL, A DUKE, AND A FRENCH POLITICIAN. NAMED CHIEF MINISTER BY LOUIS XIII, HE WAS AN EXPERT IN THE FIELD OF POLITICS AND SPENT HIS CAREER STRENGTHENING THE ROLE OF THE KING AND OF FRANCE IN EUROPE.
IF SOMETHING ODD HAS HAPPENED AT COURT, HE'LL CERTAINLY KNOW ABOUT IT.
DEFINITELY, BUT IT WON'T BE EASY TO EVEN GET NEAR HIM!
WE HAVE TO FIND A WAY TO SHOW HIM WE CAN HELP...
IF YOU'RE ONE OF HIS MUSKETEERS, HE'LL CERTAINLY LISTEN TO YOU.
MUSKETEERS?! THERE REALLY ARE MUSKETEERS HERE?!
WELL, YES. THEY'RE RICHELIEU'S PRIVATE GUARD. ACTUALLY, FROM WHAT I UNDERSTAND, THEY'RE LOOKING FOR NEW MEMBERS.
MUSKETEERS WERE A TYPE OF SOLDIER FOUND IN MANY ARMIES THROUGHOUT HISTORY. NAMED AFTER THE MUSKETS THEY USED AS WEAPONS, THESE SOLDIERS SOMETIMES CAME FROM FAMILIES WHO WERE PART OF THE LOWER NOBILITY IN FRANCE. RICHELIEU NAMED HIS PERSONAL GUARD OF MUSKET-WIELDING SOLDIERS "MUSKETEERS" AS NOT TO COMPETE WITH THE KING, WHO HAD HIS OWN ROYAL GUARD.

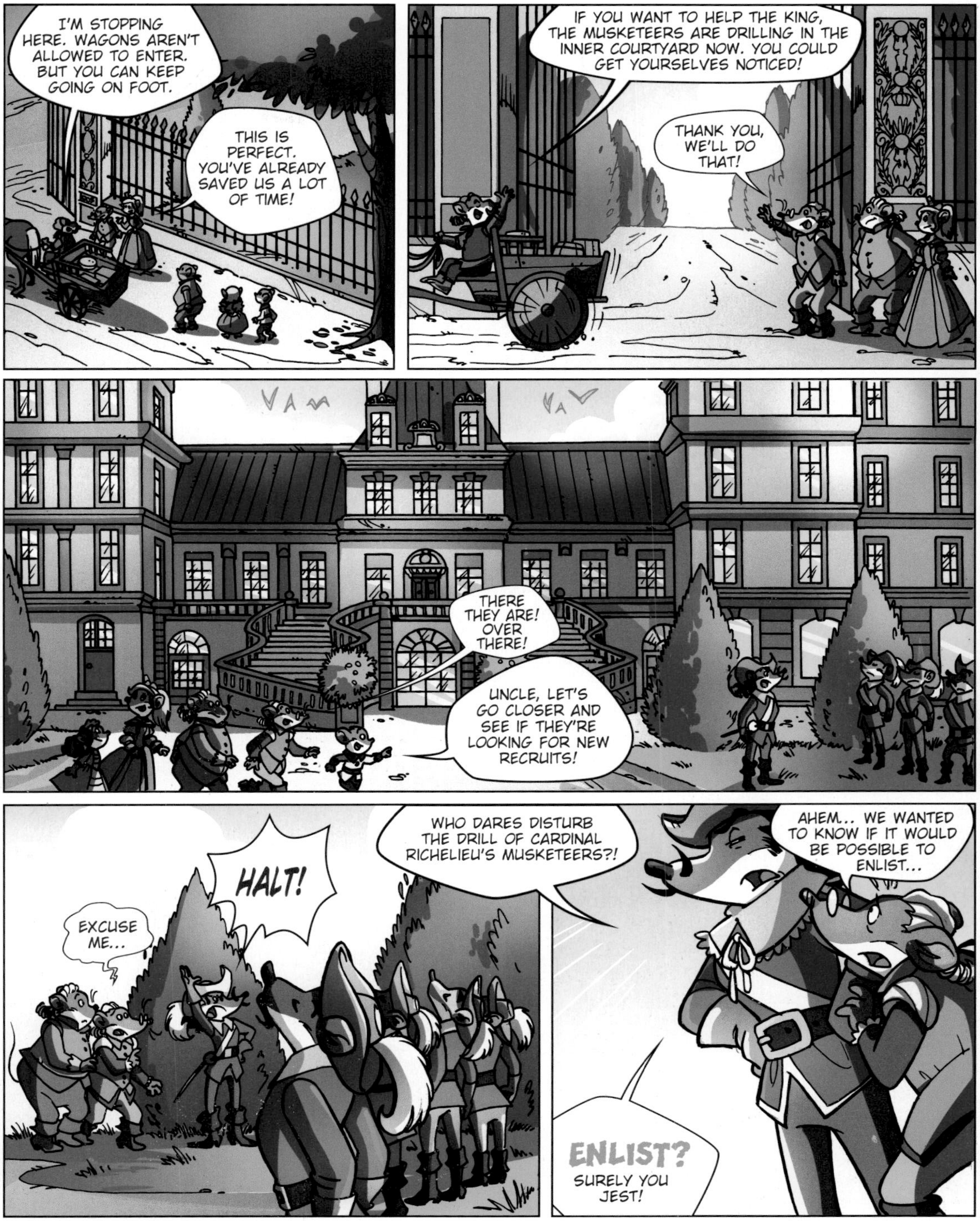
I'M STOPPING HERE. WAGONS AREN'T ALLOWED TO ENTER. BUT YOU CAN KEEP GOING ON FOOT.
THIS IS PERFECT. YOU'VE ALREADY SAVED US A LOT OF TIME!
IF YOU WANT TO HELP THE KING, THE MUSKETEERS ARE DRILLING IN THE INNER COURTYARD NOW. YOU COULD GET YOURSELVES NOTICED!
THANK YOU, WE'LL DO THAT!
THERE THEY ARE! OVER THERE!
UNCLE, LET'S GO CLOSER AND SEE IF THEY'RE LOOKING FOR NEW RECRUITS!
HALT!
EXCUSE ME...
WHO DARES DISTURB THE DRILL OF CARDINAL RICHELIEU'S MUSKETEERS?!
AHEM... WE WANTED TO KNOW IF IT WOULD BE POSSIBLE TO ENLIST...
ENLIST? SURELY YOU JEST!

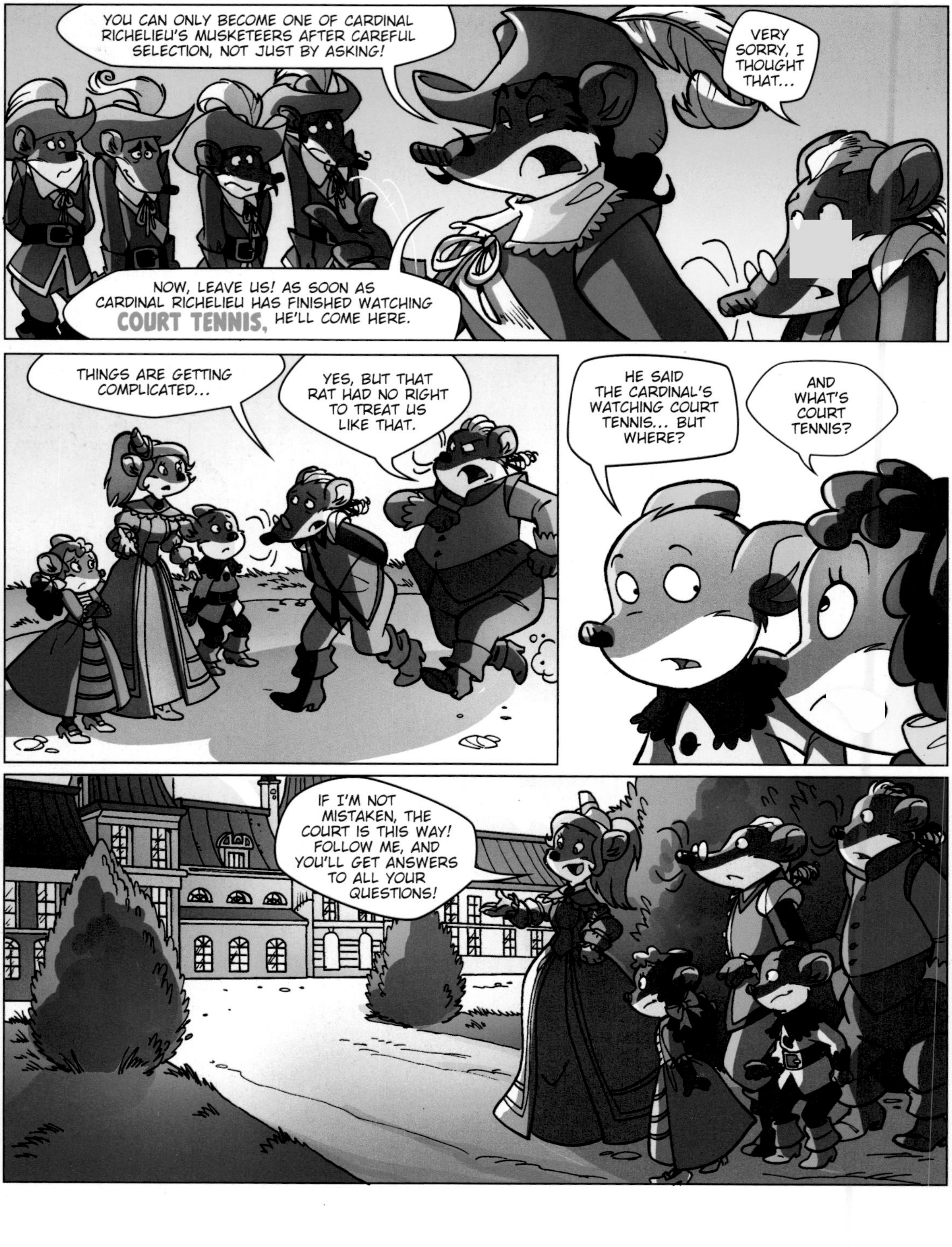
YOU CAN ONLY BECOME ONE OF CARDINAL RICHELIEU'S MUSKETEERS AFTER CAREFUL SELECTION, NOT JUST BY ASKING!
VERY SORRY, I THOUGHT THAT...
NOW, LEAVE US! AS SOON AS CARDINAL RICHELIEU HAS FINISHED WATCHING COURT TENNIS, HE'LL COME HERE.
THINGS ARE GETTING COMPLICATED...
YES, BUT THAT RAT HAD NO RIGHT TO TREAT US LIKE THAT.
HE SAID THE CARDINAL'S WATCHING COURT TENNIS... BUT WHERE?
AND WHAT'S COURT TENNIS?
IF I'M NOT MISTAKEN, THE COURT IS THIS WAY! FOLLOW ME, AND YOU'LL GET ANSWERS TO ALL YOUR QUESTIONS!

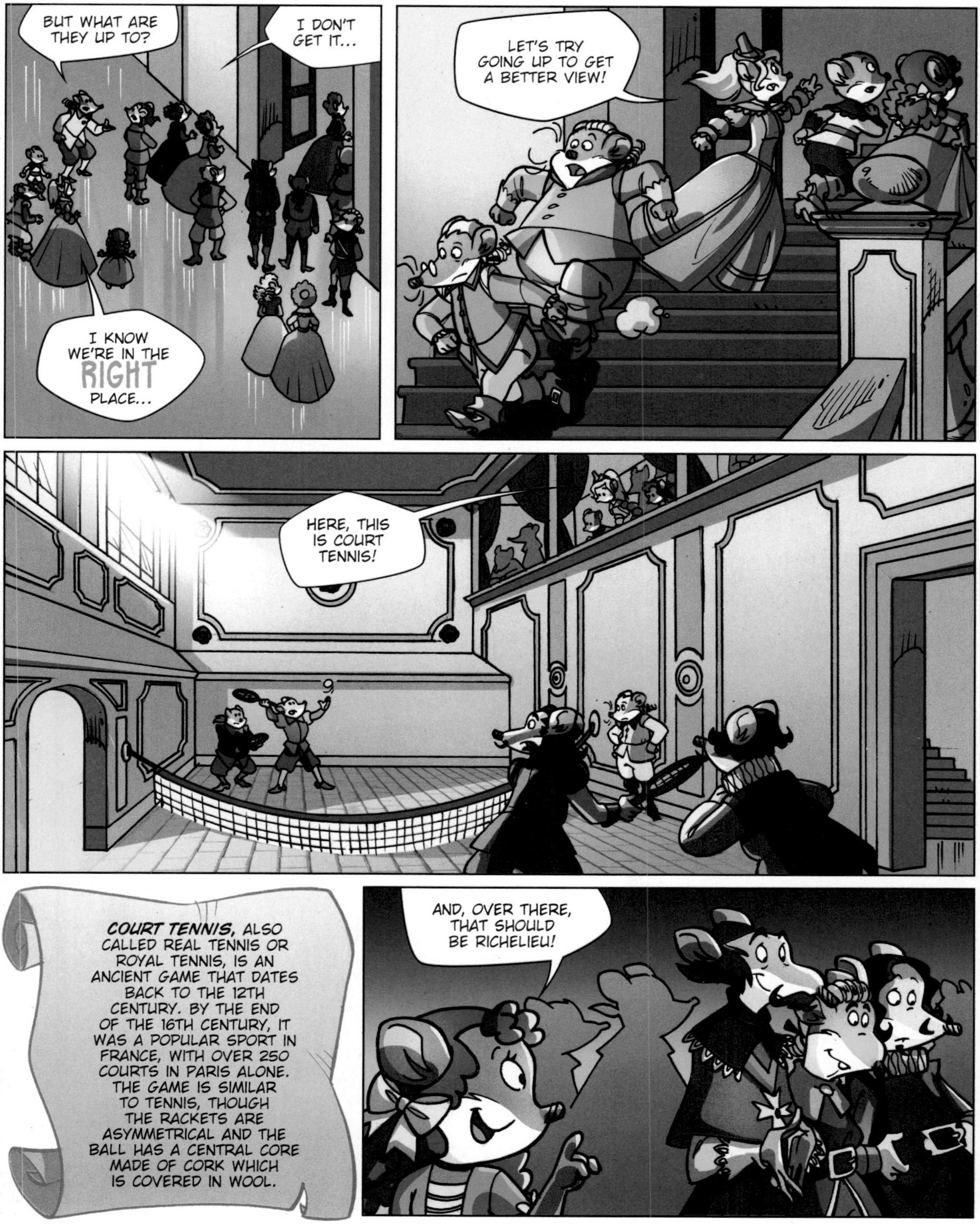
BUT WHAT ARE THEY UP TO?
I DON'T GET IT...
I KNOW WE'RE IN THE RIGHT PLACE...
LET'S TRY GOING UP TO GET A BETTER VIEW!
HERE, THIS IS COURT TENNIS!
COURT TENNIS, ALSO CALLED REAL TENNIS OR ROYAL TENNIS, IS AN ANCIENT GAME THAT DATES BACK TO THE 12TH CENTURY. BY THE END OF THE 16TH CENTURY, IT WAS A POPULAR SPORT IN FRANCE, WITH OVER 250 COURTS IN PARIS ALONE. THE GAME IS SIMILAR TO TENNIS, THOUGH THE RACKETS ARE ASYMMETRICAL AND THE BALL HAS A CENTRAL CORE MADE OF CORK WHICH IS COVERED IN WOOL.
AND, OVER THERE, THAT SHOULD BE RICHELIEU!

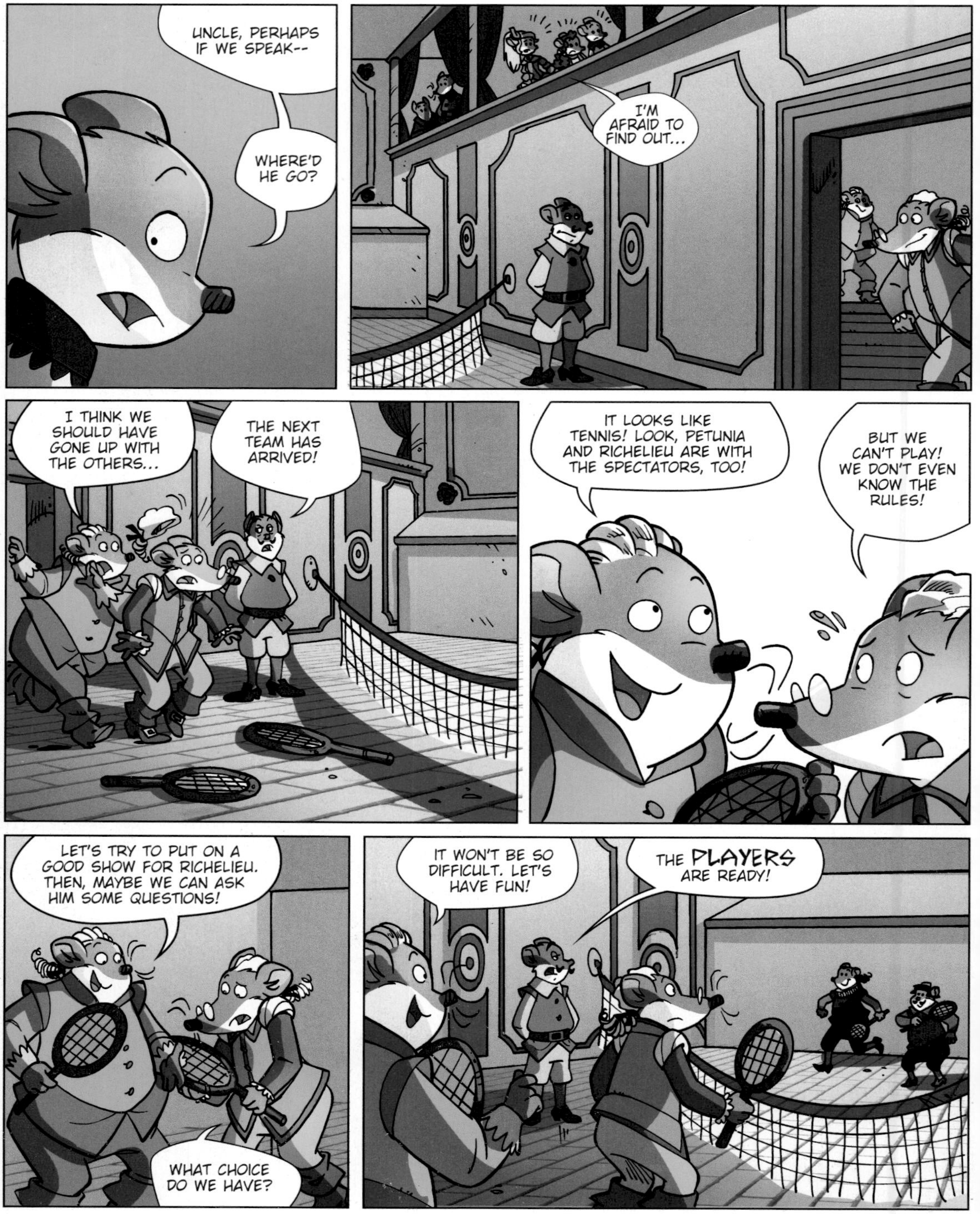
UNCLE, PERHAPS IF WE SPEAK--
WHERE'D HE GO?
I'M AFRAID TO FIND OUT...
I THINK WE SHOULD HAVE GONE UP WITH THE OTHERS...
THE NEXT TEAM HAS ARRIVED!
IT LOOKS LIKE TENNIS! LOOK, PETUNIA AND RICHELIEU ARE WITH THE SPECTATORS, TOO!
BUT WE CAN'T PLAY! WE DON'T EVEN KNOW THE RULES!
LET'S TRY TO PUT ON A GOOD SHOW FOR RICHELIEU. THEN, MAYBE WE CAN ASK HIM SOME QUESTIONS!
WHAT CHOICE DO WE HAVE?
IT WON'T BE SO DIFFICULT. LET'S HAVE FUN!
THE PLAYERS ARE READY!

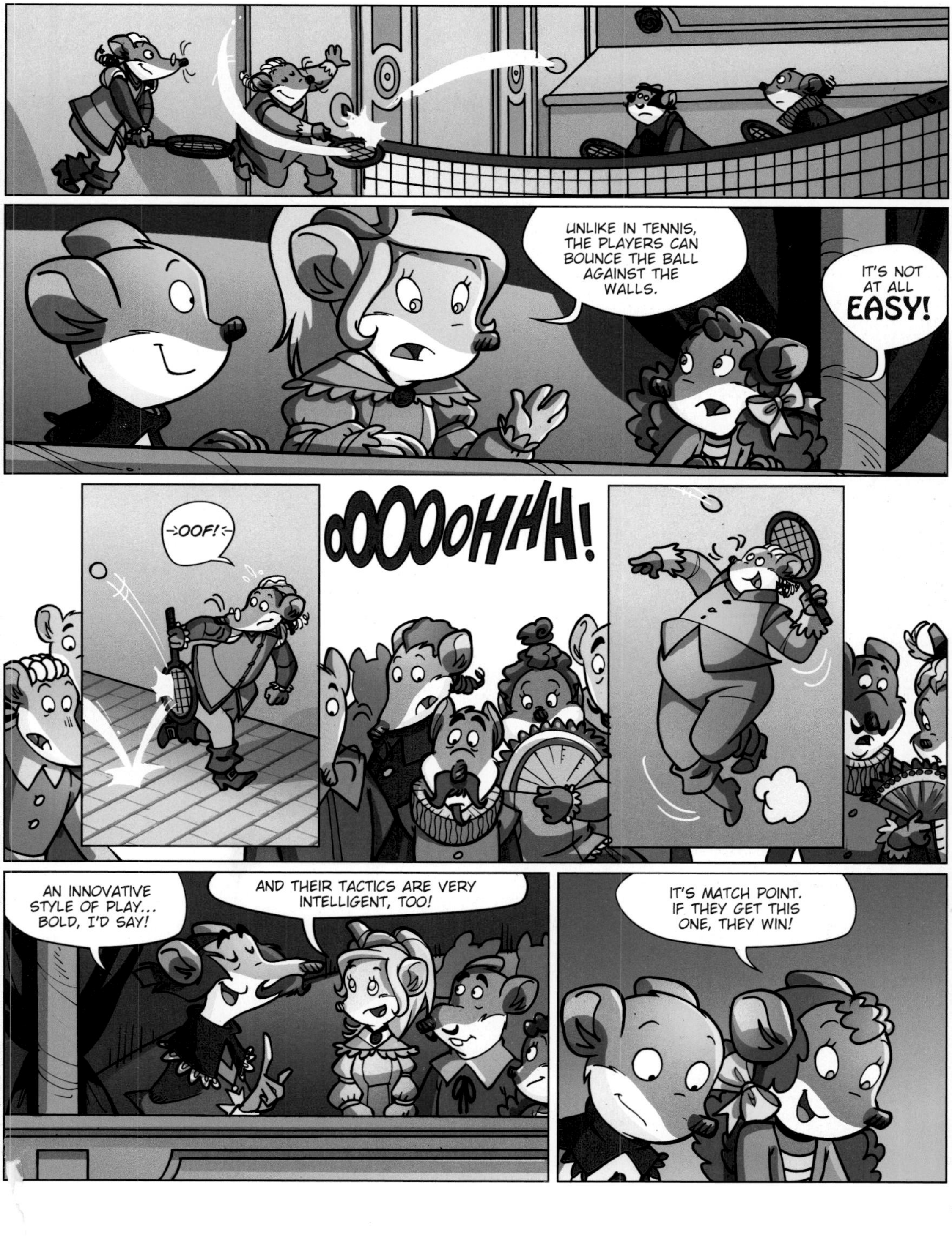
UNLIKE IN TENNIS, THE PLAYERS CAN BOUNCE THE BALL AGAINST THE WALLS.
IT'S NOT AT ALL EASY!
OOF!
OOOOOHHH!
AN INNOVATIVE STYLE OF PLAY... BOLD, I'D SAY!
AND THEIR TACTICS ARE VERY INTELLIGENT, TOO!
IT'S MATCH POINT. IF THEY GET THIS ONE, THEY WIN!

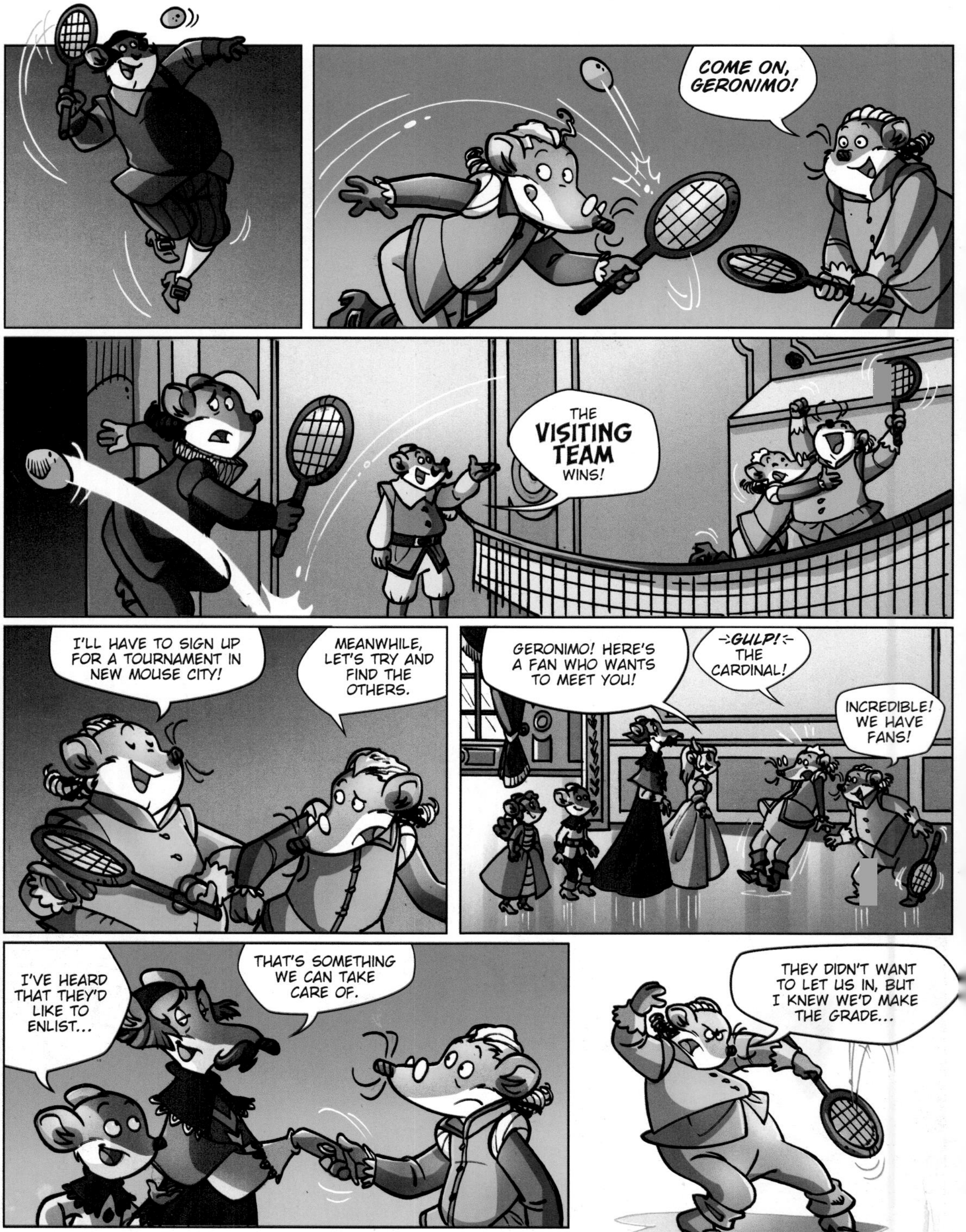
COME ON, GERONIMO!
THE VISITING TEAM WINS!
I'LL HAVE TO SIGN UP FOR A TOURNAMENT IN NEW MOUSE CITY!
MEANWHILE, LET'S TRY AND FIND THE OTHERS.
GERONIMO! HERE'S A FAN WHO WANTS TO MEET YOU!
GULP! THE CARDINAL!
INCREDIBLE! WE HAVE FANS!
I'VE HEARD THAT THEY'D LIKE TO ENLIST...
THAT'S SOMETHING WE CAN TAKE CARE OF.
THEY DIDN'T WANT TO LET US IN, BUT I KNEW WE'D MAKE THE GRADE...

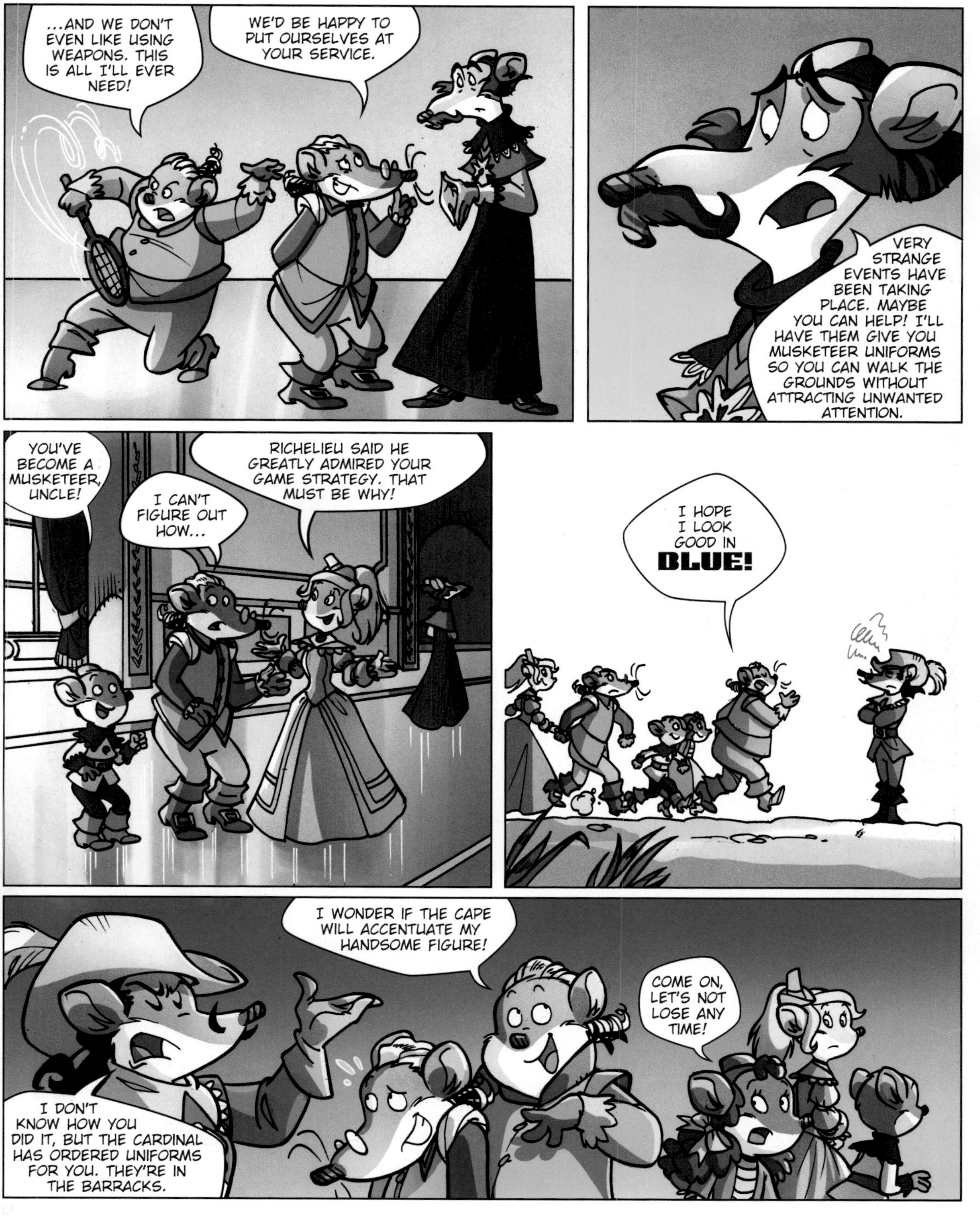
...AND WE DON'T EVEN LIKE USING WEAPONS. THIS IS ALL I'LL EVER NEED!
WE'D BE HAPPY TO PUT OURSELVES AT YOUR SERVICE.
VERY STRANGE EVENTS HAVE BEEN TAKING PLACE. MAYBE YOU CAN HELP! I'LL HAVE THEM GIVE YOU MUSKETEER UNIFORMS SO YOU CAN WALK THE GROUNDS WITHOUT ATTRACTING UNWANTED ATTENTION.
YOU'VE BECOME A MUSKETEER, UNCLE!
I CAN'T FIGURE OUT HOW...
RICHELIEU SAID HE GREATLY ADMIRED YOUR GAME STRATEGY. THAT MUST BE WHY!
I HOPE I LOOK GOOD IN BLUE!
I DON'T KNOW HOW YOU DID IT, BUT THE CARDINAL HAS ORDERED UNIFORMS FOR YOU. THEY'RE IN THE BARRACKS.
I WONDER IF THE CAPE WILL ACCENTUATE MY HANDSOME FIGURE!
COME ON, LET'S NOT LOSE ANY TIME!

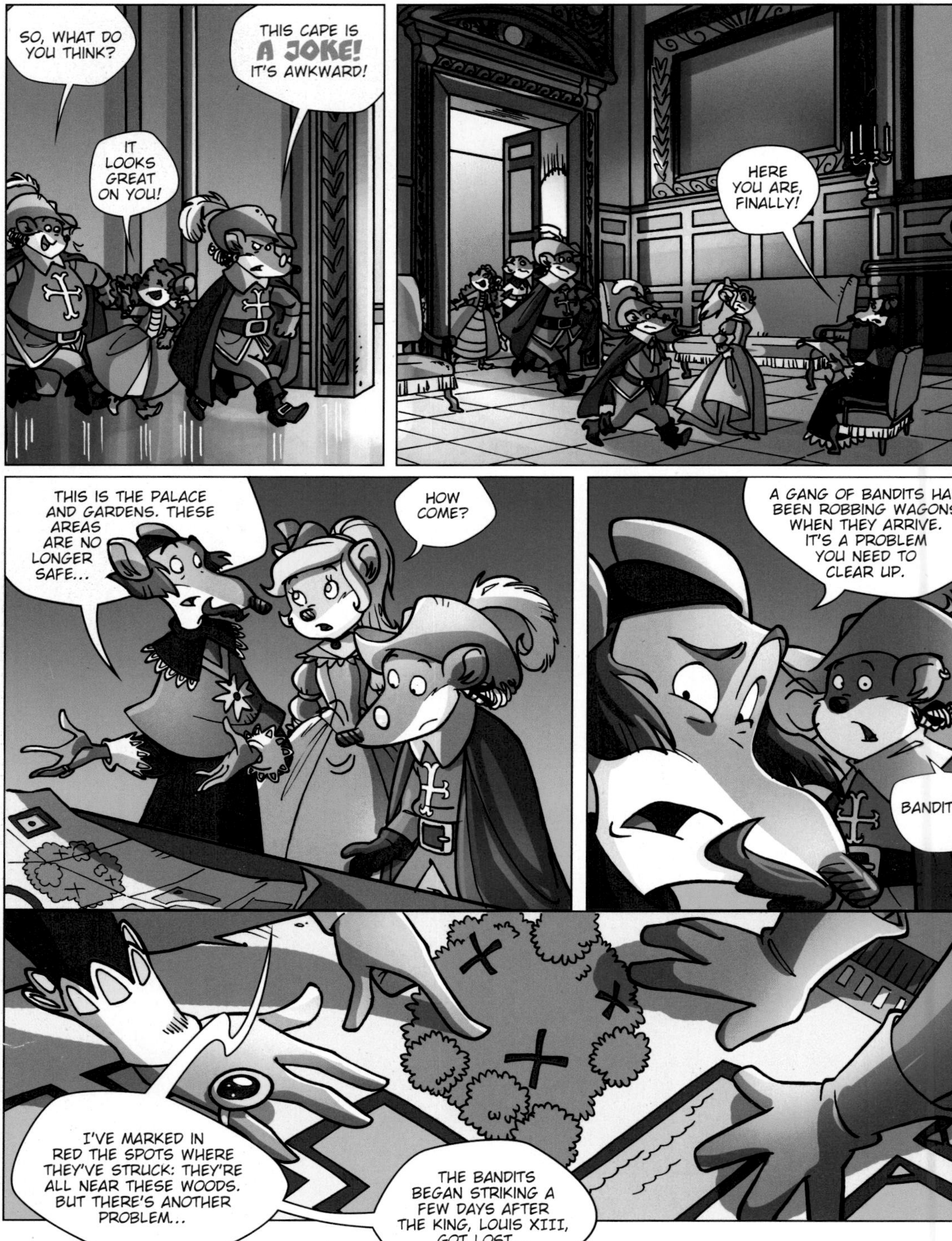
SO, WHAT DO YOU THINK?
IT LOOKS GREAT ON YOU!
THIS CAPE IS A JOKE! IT'S AWKWARD!
HERE YOU ARE, FINALLY!
THIS IS THE PALACE AND GARDENS. THESE AREAS ARE NO LONGER SAFE...
HOW COME?
A GANG OF BANDITS HAS BEEN ROBBING WAGONS WHEN THEY ARRIVE. IT'S A PROBLEM YOU NEED TO CLEAR UP.
BANDITS?
I'VE MARKED IN RED THE SPOTS WHERE THEY'VE STRUCK: THEY'RE ALL NEAR THESE WOODS. BUT THERE'S ANOTHER PROBLEM...
THE BANDITS BEGAN STRIKING A FEW DAYS AFTER THE KING, LOUIS XIII, GOT LOST...

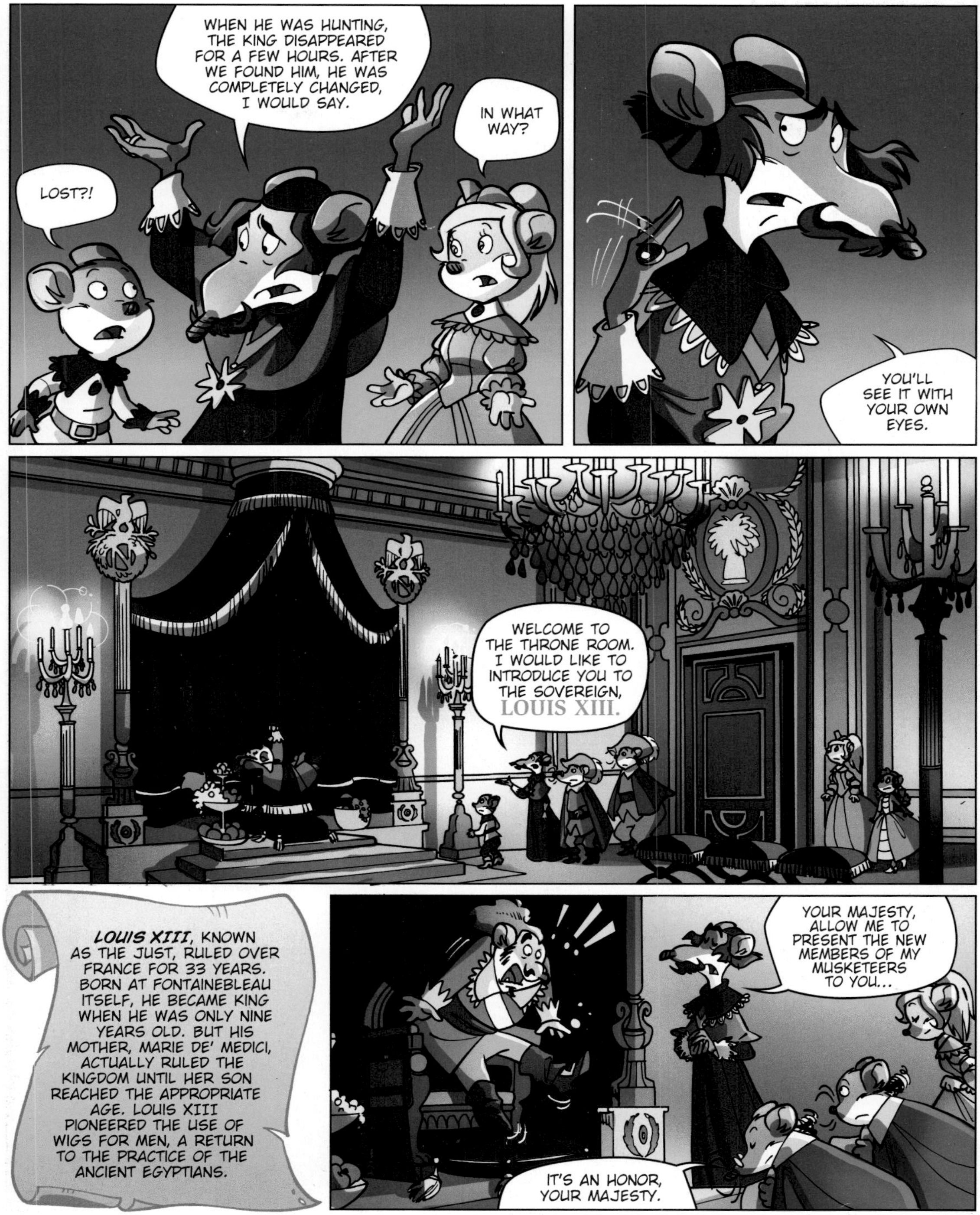
LOST?!
WHEN HE WAS HUNTING, THE KING DISAPPEARED FOR A FEW HOURS. AFTER WE FOUND HIM, HE WAS COMPLETELY CHANGED, I WOULD SAY.
IN WHAT WAY?
YOU'LL SEE IT WITH YOUR OWN EYES.
WELCOME TO THE THRONE ROOM. I WOULD LIKE TO INTRODUCE YOU TO THE SOVEREIGN, LOUIS XIII.
LOUIS XIII, KNOWN AS THE JUST, RULED OVER FRANCE FOR 33 YEARS. BORN AT FONTAINEBLEAU ITSELF, HE BECAME KING WHEN HE WAS ONLY NINE YEARS OLD. BUT HIS MOTHER, MARIE DE' MEDICI, ACTUALLY RULED THE KINGDOM UNTIL HER SON REACHED THE APPROPRIATE AGE. LOUIS XIII PIONEERED THE USE OF WIGS FOR MEN, A RETURN TO THE PRACTICE OF THE ANCIENT EGYPTIANS.
YOUR MAJESTY, ALLOW ME TO PRESENT THE NEW MEMBERS OF MY MUSKETEERS TO YOU...
IT'S AN HONOR, YOUR MAJESTY.

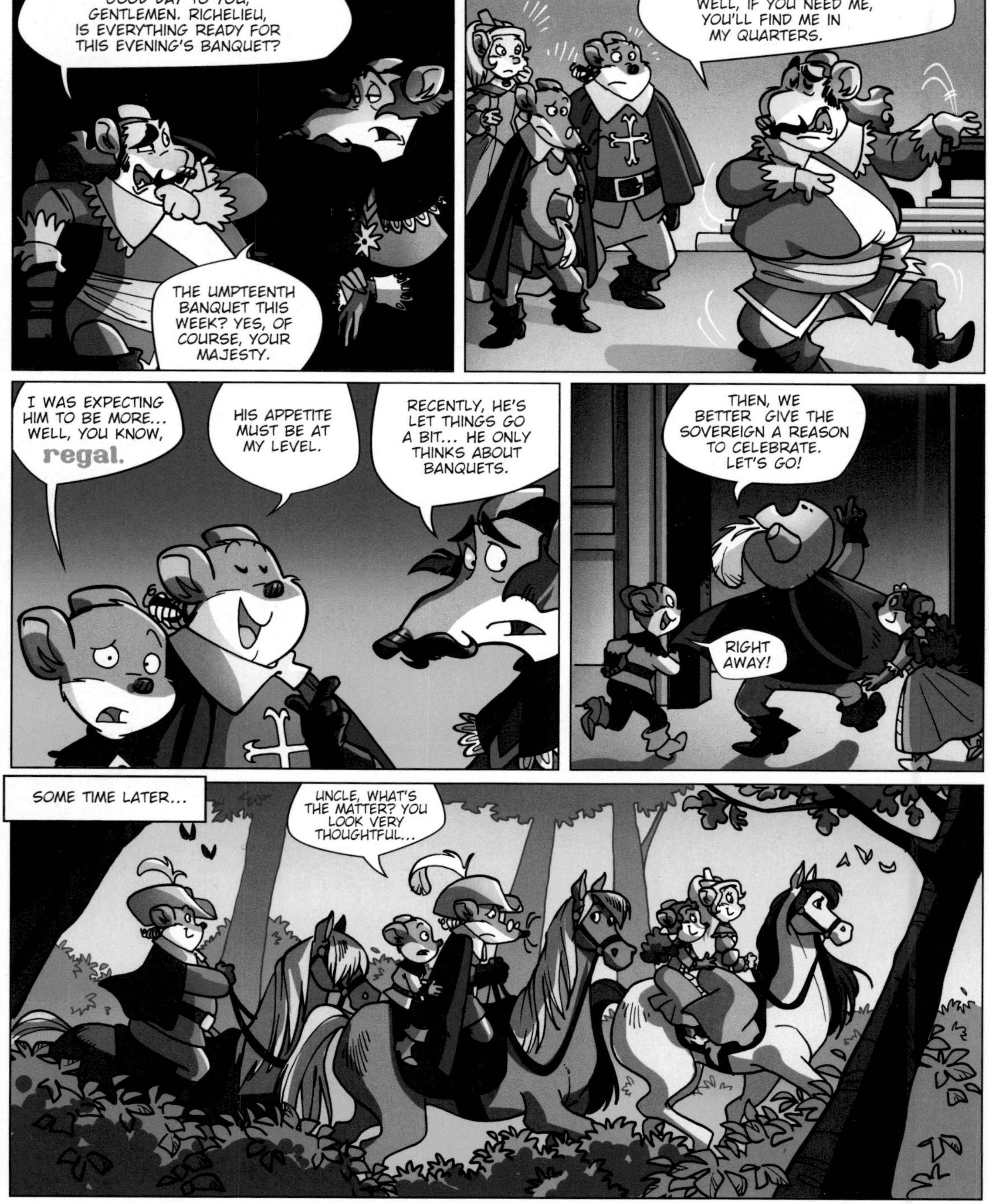
GOOD DAY TO YOU, GENTLEMEN. RICHELIEU, IS EVERYTHING READY FOR THIS EVENING'S BANQUET?
THE UMPTEENTH BANQUET THIS WEEK? YES, OF COURSE, YOUR MAJESTY.
WELL, IF YOU NEED ME, YOU'LL FIND ME IN MY QUARTERS.
I WAS EXPECTING HIM TO BE MORE... WELL, YOU KNOW, regal.
HIS APPETITE MUST BE AT MY LEVEL.
RECENTLY, HE'S LET THINGS GO A BIT... HE ONLY THINKS ABOUT BANQUETS.
THEN, WE BETTER GIVE THE SOVEREIGN A REASON TO CELEBRATE. LET'S GO!
RIGHT AWAY!
SOME TIME LATER...
UNCLE, WHAT'S THE MATTER? YOU LOOK VERY THOUGHTFUL...

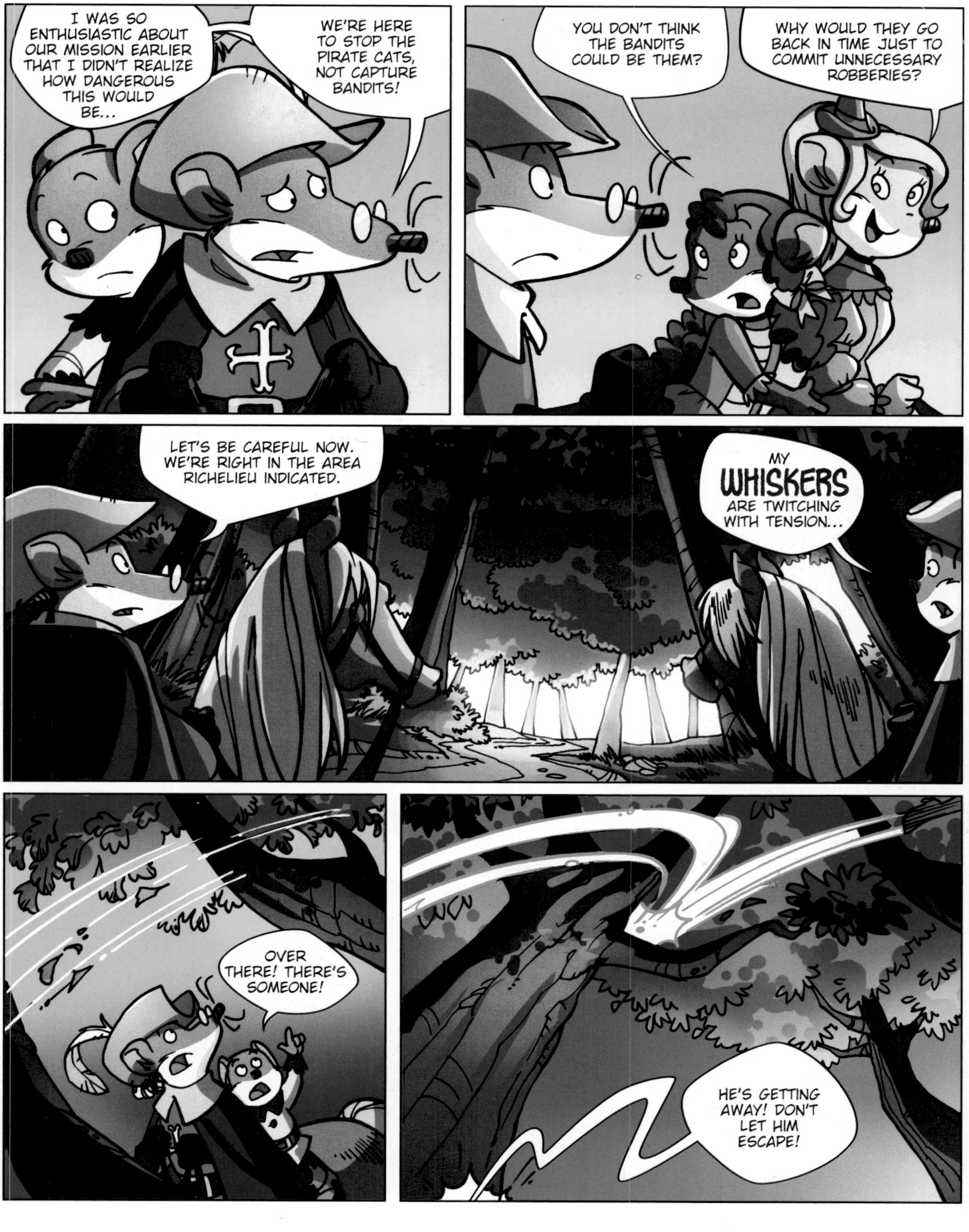
I WAS SO ENTHUSIASTIC ABOUT OUR MISSION EARLIER THAT I DIDN'T REALIZE HOW DANGEROUS THIS WOULD BE...
WE'RE HERE TO STOP THE PIRATE CATS, NOT CAPTURE BANDITS!
YOU DON'T THINK THE BANDITS COULD BE THEM?
WHY WOULD THEY GO BACK IN TIME JUST TO COMMIT UNNECESSARY ROBBERIES?
LET'S BE CAREFUL NOW. WE'RE RIGHT IN THE AREA RICHELIEU INDICATED.
MY WHISKERS ARE TWITCHING WITH TENSION...
OVER THERE! THERE'S SOMEONE!
HE'S GETTING AWAY! DON'T LET HIM ESCAPE!

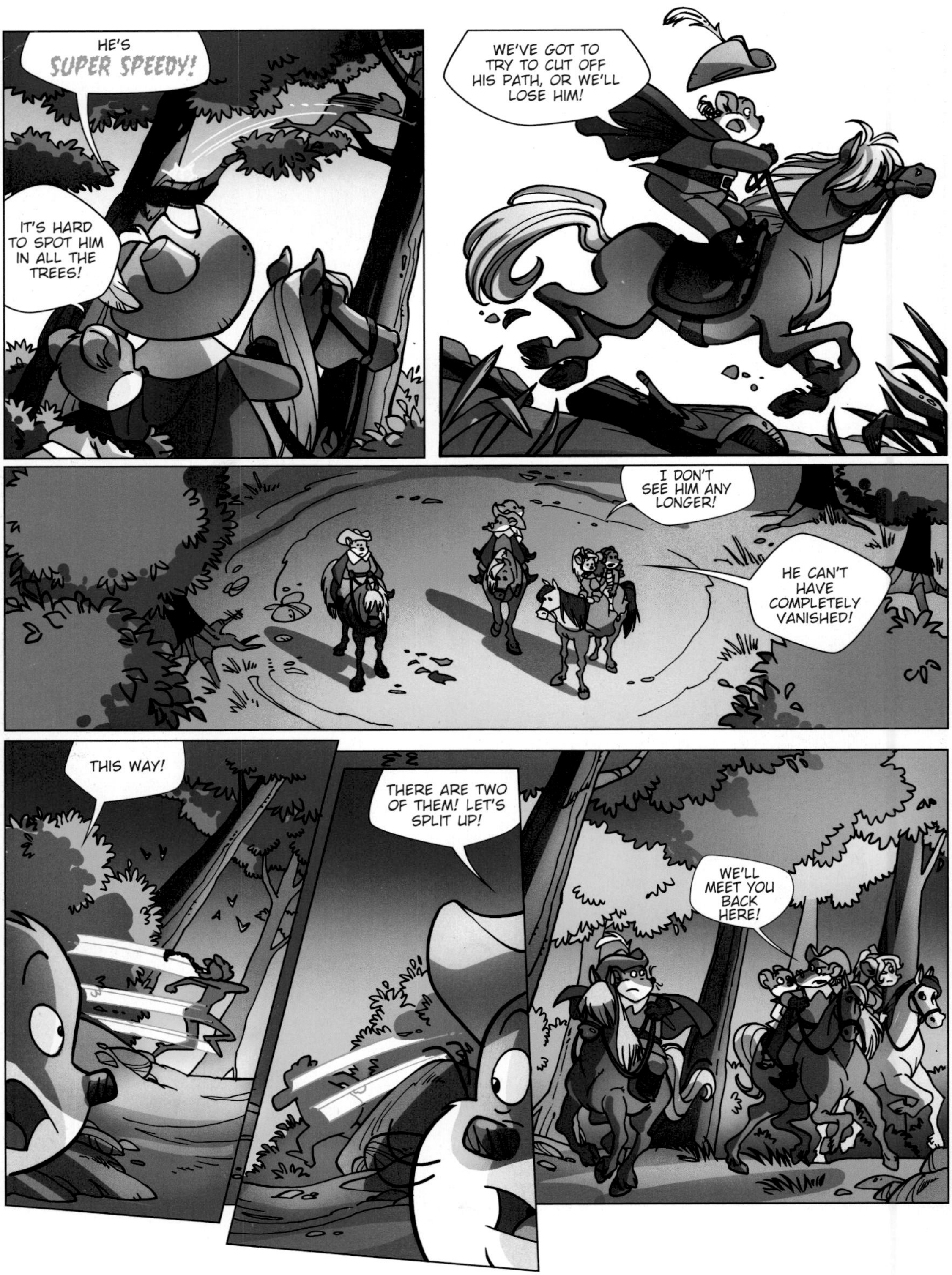
HE'S SUPER SPEEDY!
IT'S HARD TO SPOT HIM IN ALL THE TREES!
WE'VE GOT TO TRY TO CUT OFF HIS PATH, OR WE'LL LOSE HIM!
I DON'T SEE HIM ANY LONGER!
HE CAN'T HAVE COMPLETELY VANISHED!
THIS WAY!
THERE ARE TWO OF THEM! LET'S SPLIT UP!
WE'LL MEET YOU BACK HERE!

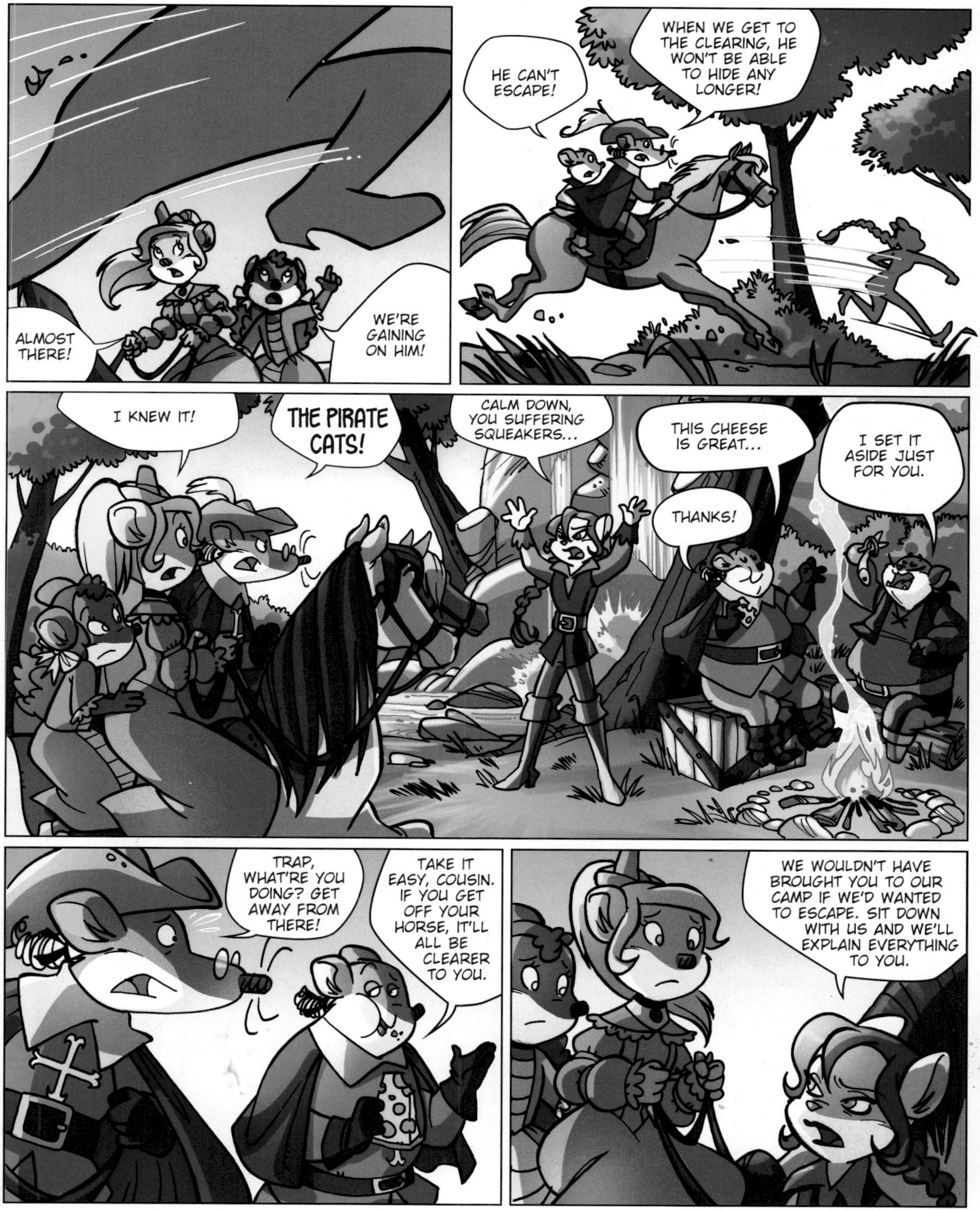
ALMOST THERE!
WE'RE GAINING ON HIM!
HE CAN'T ESCAPE!
WHEN WE GET TO THE CLEARING, HE WON'T BE ABLE TO HIDE ANY LONGER!
I KNEW IT!
THE PIRATE CATS!
CALM DOWN, YOU SUFFERING SQUEAKERS...
THIS CHEESE IS GREAT...
THANKS!
I SET IT ASIDE JUST FOR YOU.
TRAP, WHAT'RE YOU DOING? GET AWAY FROM THERE!
TAKE IT EASY, COUSIN. IF YOU GET OFF YOUR HORSE, IT'LL ALL BE CLEARER TO YOU.
WE WOULDN'T HAVE BROUGHT YOU TO OUR CAMP IF WE'D WANTED TO ESCAPE. SIT DOWN WITH US AND WE'LL EXPLAIN EVERYTHING TO YOU.

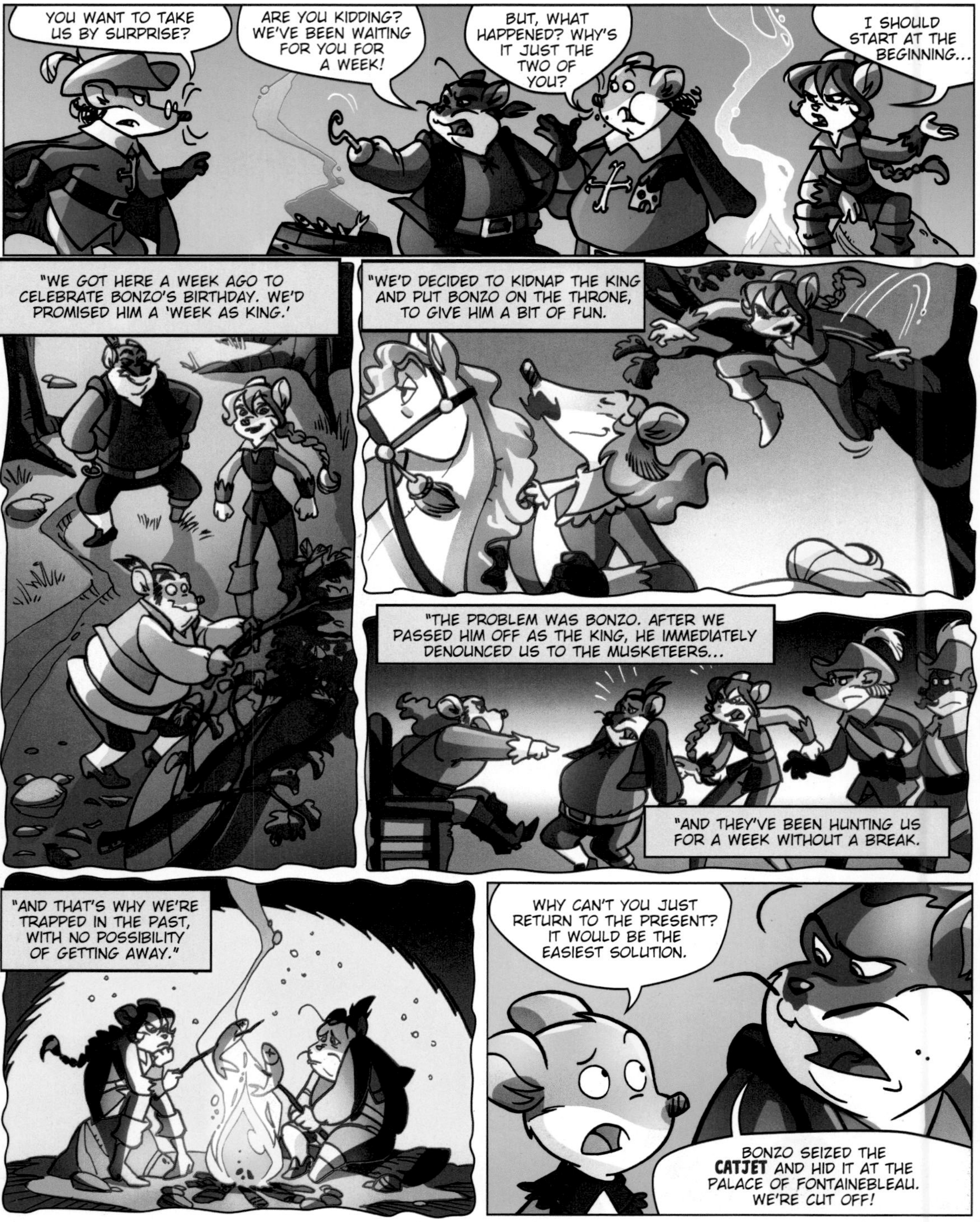
YOU WANT TO TAKE US BY SURPRISE?
ARE YOU KIDDING? WE'VE BEEN WAITING FOR YOU FOR A WEEK!
BUT, WHAT HAPPENED? WHY'S IT JUST THE TWO OF YOU?
I SHOULD START AT THE BEGINNING...
"WE GOT HERE A WEEK AGO TO CELEBRATE BONZO'S BIRTHDAY. WE'D PROMISED HIM A 'WEEK AS KING.'
"WE'D DECIDED TO KIDNAP THE KING AND PUT BONZO ON THE THRONE, TO GIVE HIM A BIT OF FUN.
"THE PROBLEM WAS BONZO. AFTER WE PASSED HIM OFF AS THE KING, HE IMMEDIATELY DENOUNCED US TO THE MUSKETEERS...
"AND THEY'VE BEEN HUNTING US FOR A WEEK WITHOUT A BREAK.
"AND THAT'S WHY WE'RE TRAPPED IN THE PAST, WITH NO POSSIBILITY OF GETTING AWAY."
WHY CAN'T YOU JUST RETURN TO THE PRESENT? IT WOULD BE THE EASIEST SOLUTION.
BONZO SEIZED THE **CATJET** AND HID IT AT THE PALACE OF FONTAINEBLEAU. WE'RE CUT OFF!

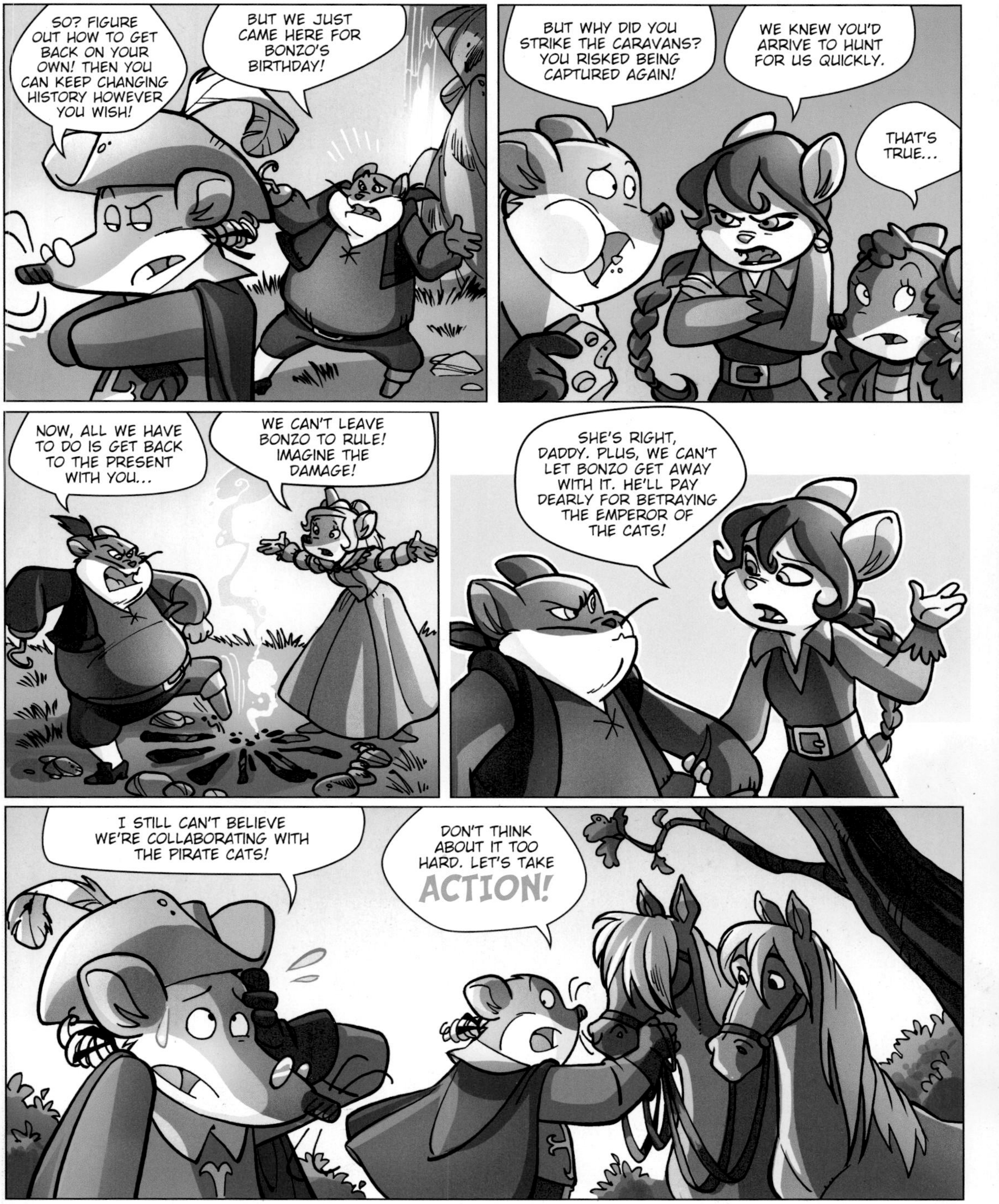
SO? FIGURE OUT HOW TO GET BACK ON YOUR OWN! THEN YOU CAN KEEP CHANGING HISTORY HOWEVER YOU WISH!
BUT WE JUST CAME HERE FOR BONZO'S BIRTHDAY!
BUT WHY DID YOU STRIKE THE CARAVANS? YOU RISKED BEING CAPTURED AGAIN!
WE KNEW YOU'D ARRIVE TO HUNT FOR US QUICKLY.
THAT'S TRUE...
NOW, ALL WE HAVE TO DO IS GET BACK TO THE PRESENT WITH YOU...
WE CAN'T LEAVE BONZO TO RULE! IMAGINE THE DAMAGE!
SHE'S RIGHT, DADDY. PLUS, WE CAN'T LET BONZO GET AWAY WITH IT. HE'LL PAY DEARLY FOR BETRAYING THE EMPEROR OF THE CATS!
I STILL CAN'T BELIEVE WE'RE COLLABORATING WITH THE PIRATE CATS!
DON'T THINK ABOUT IT TOO HARD. LET'S TAKE ACTION!

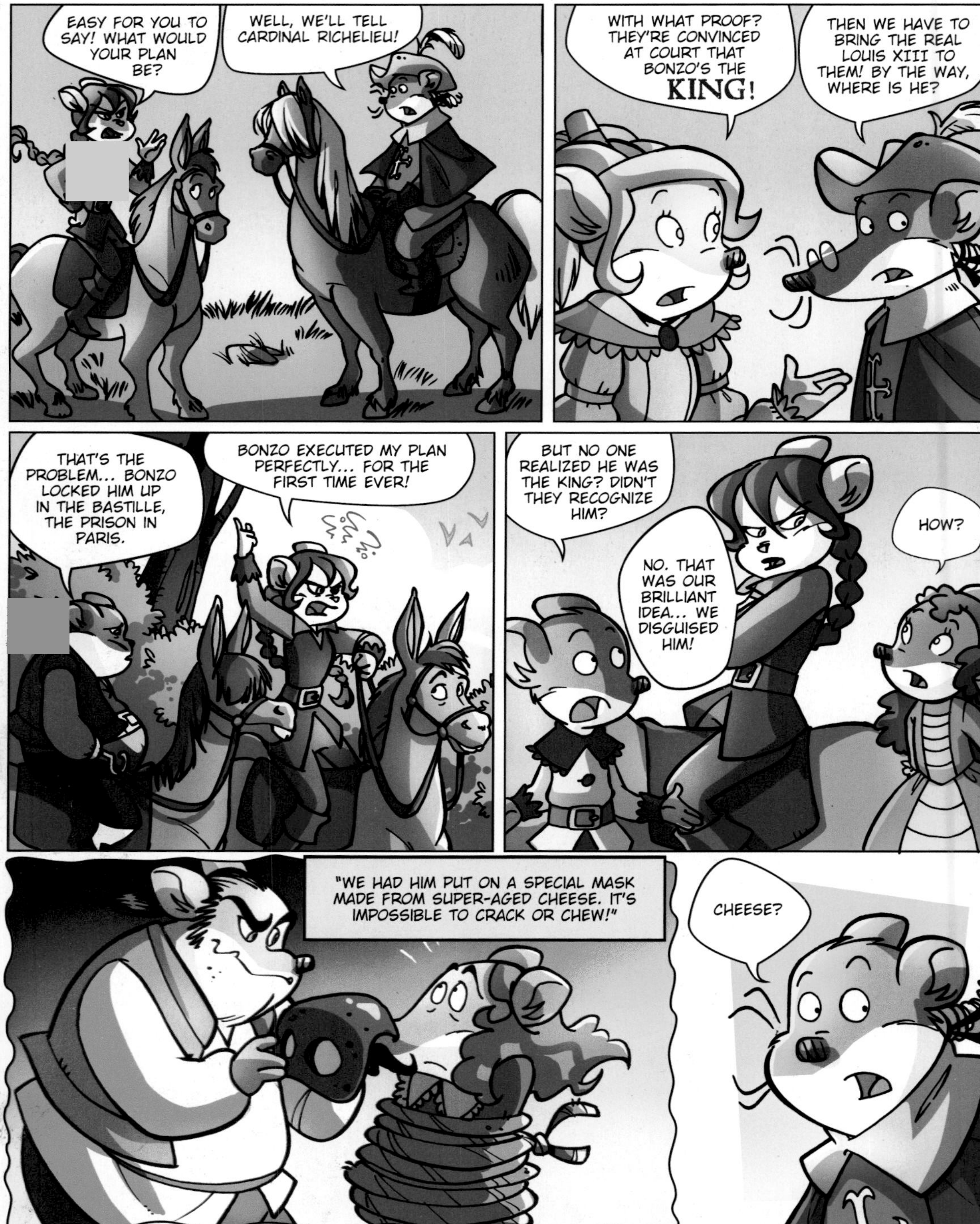

EASY FOR YOU TO SAY! WHAT WOULD YOUR PLAN BE?
WELL, WE'LL TELL CARDINAL RICHELIEU!
WITH WHAT PROOF? THEY'RE CONVINCED AT COURT THAT BONZO'S THE KING!
THEN WE HAVE TO BRING THE REAL LOUIS XIII TO THEM! BY THE WAY, WHERE IS HE?
THAT'S THE PROBLEM... BONZO LOCKED HIM UP IN THE BASTILLE, THE PRISON IN PARIS.
BONZO EXECUTED MY PLAN PERFECTLY... FOR THE FIRST TIME EVER!
BUT NO ONE REALIZED HE WAS THE KING? DIDN'T THEY RECOGNIZE HIM?
NO. THAT WAS OUR BRILLIANT IDEA... WE DISGUISED HIM!
HOW?
"WE HAD HIM PUT ON A SPECIAL MASK MADE FROM SUPER-AGED CHEESE. IT'S IMPOSSIBLE TO CRACK OR CHEW!"
CHEESE?

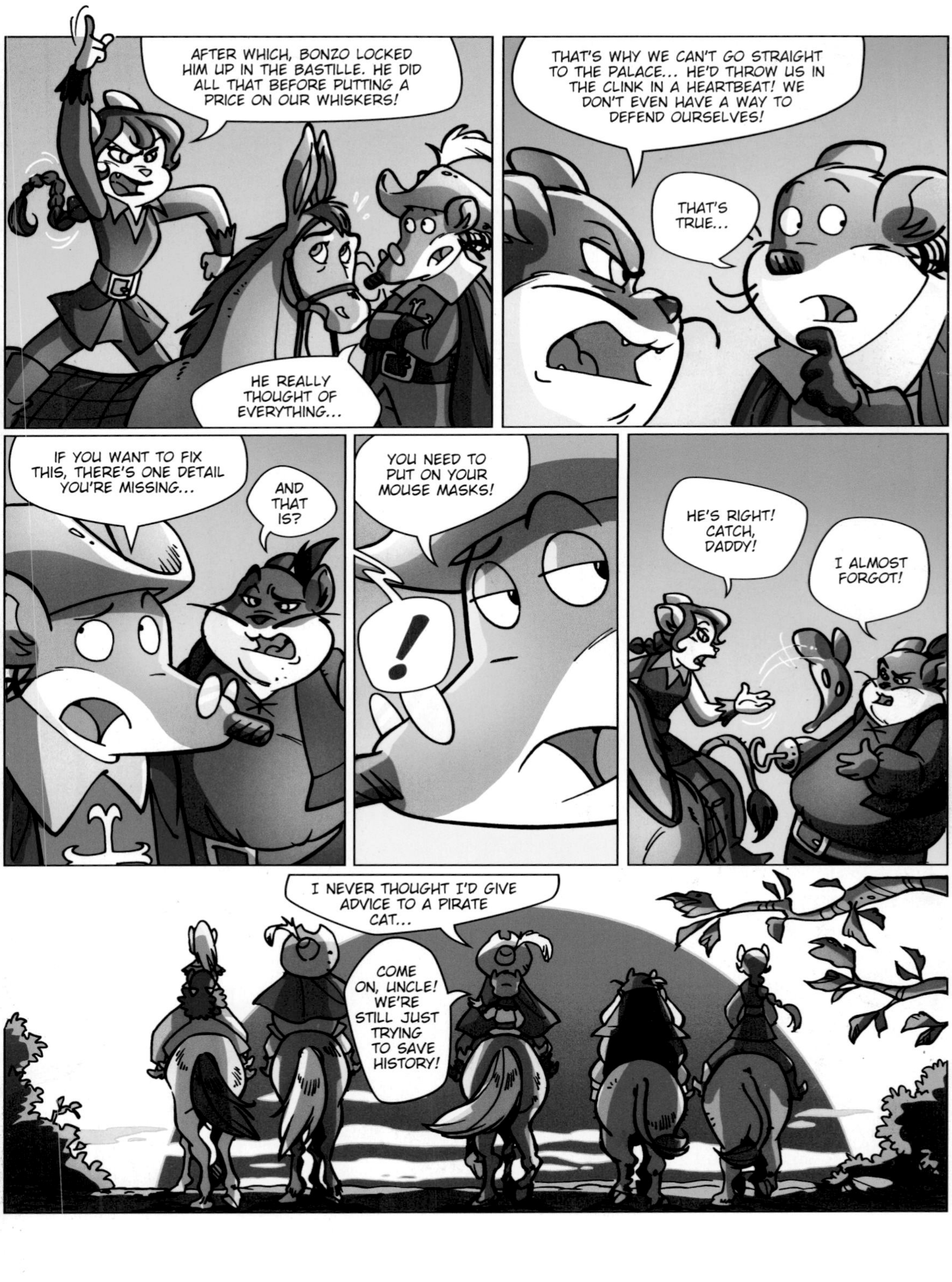
AFTER WHICH, BONZO LOCKED HIM UP IN THE BASTILLE. HE DID ALL THAT BEFORE PUTTING A PRICE ON OUR WHISKERS!
HE REALLY THOUGHT OF EVERYTHING...
THAT'S WHY WE CAN'T GO STRAIGHT TO THE PALACE... HE'D THROW US IN THE CLINK IN A HEARTBEAT! WE DON'T EVEN HAVE A WAY TO DEFEND OURSELVES!
THAT'S TRUE...
IF YOU WANT TO FIX THIS, THERE'S ONE DETAIL YOU'RE MISSING...
AND THAT IS?
YOU NEED TO PUT ON YOUR MOUSE MASKS!
!
HE'S RIGHT! CATCH, DADDY!
I ALMOST FORGOT!
I NEVER THOUGHT I'D GIVE ADVICE TO A PIRATE CAT...
COME ON, UNCLE! WE'RE STILL JUST TRYING TO SAVE HISTORY!

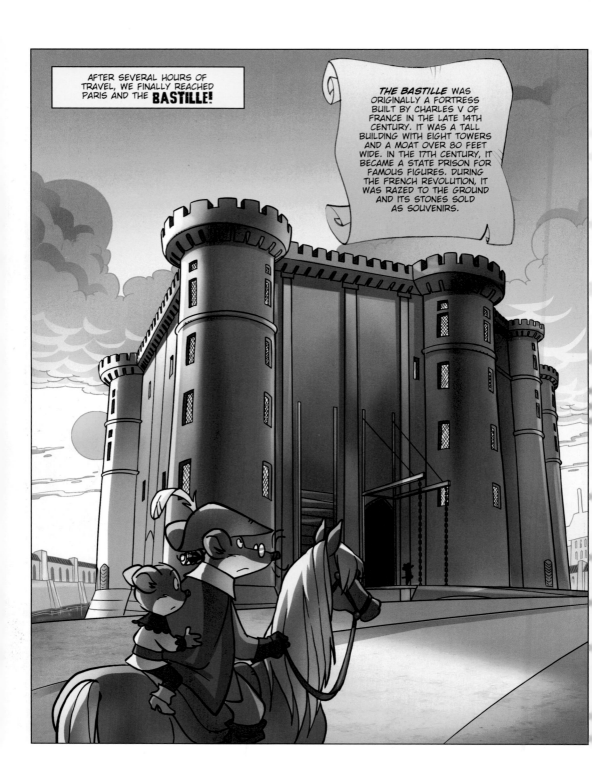

AFTER SEVERAL HOURS OF TRAVEL, WE FINALLY REACHED PARIS AND THE **BASTILLE!**

THE BASTILLE WAS ORIGINALLY A FORTRESS BUILT BY CHARLES V OF FRANCE IN THE LATE 14TH CENTURY. IT WAS A TALL BUILDING WITH EIGHT TOWERS AND A MOAT OVER 80 FEET WIDE. IN THE 17TH CENTURY, IT BECAME A STATE PRISON FOR FAMOUS FIGURES. DURING THE FRENCH REVOLUTION, IT WAS RAZED TO THE GROUND AND ITS STONES SOLD AS SOUVENIRS.

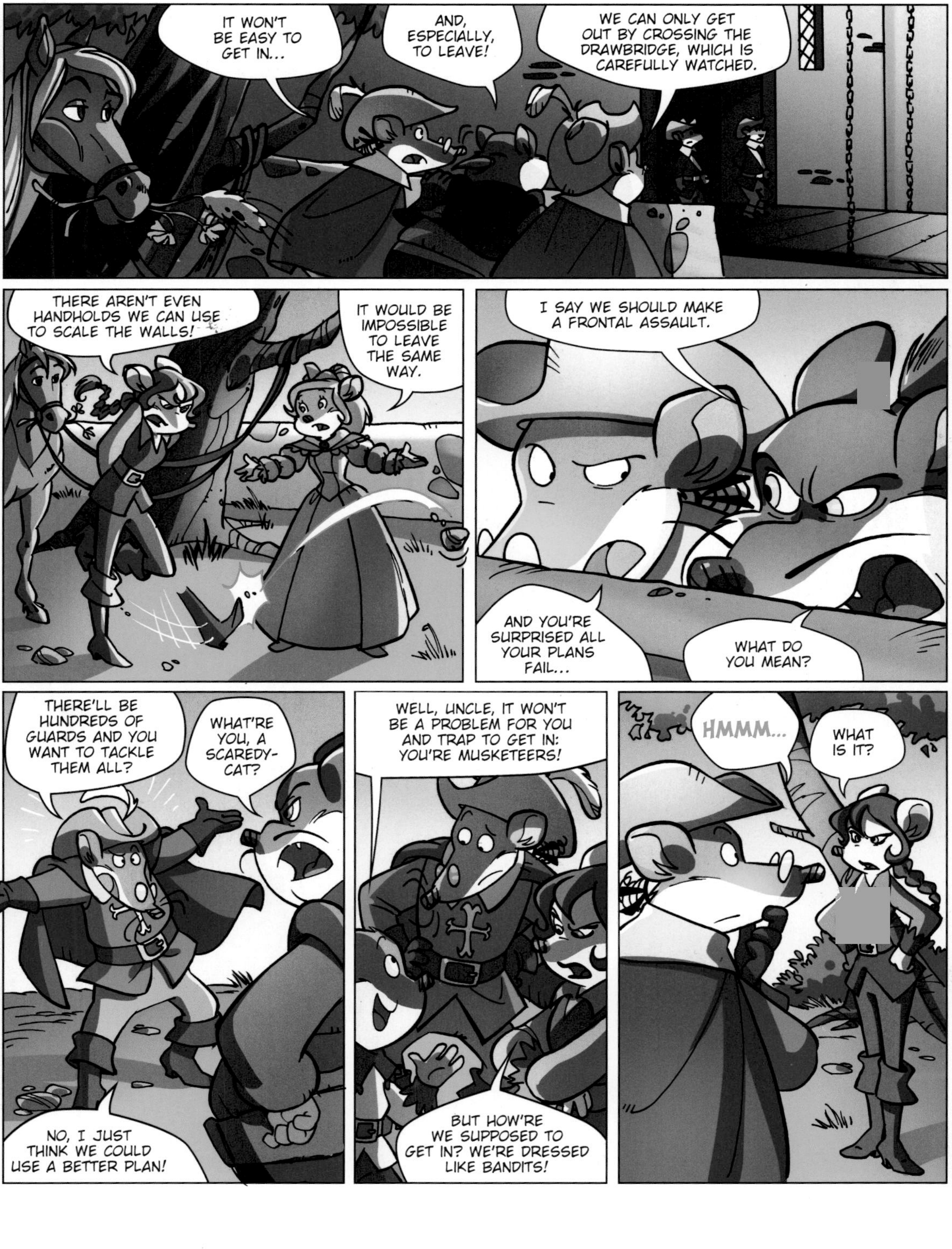
IT WON'T BE EASY TO GET IN...
AND, ESPECIALLY, TO LEAVE!
WE CAN ONLY GET OUT BY CROSSING THE DRAWBRIDGE, WHICH IS CAREFULLY WATCHED.
THERE AREN'T EVEN HANDHOLDS WE CAN USE TO SCALE THE WALLS!
IT WOULD BE IMPOSSIBLE TO LEAVE THE SAME WAY.
I SAY WE SHOULD MAKE A FRONTAL ASSAULT.
AND YOU'RE SURPRISED ALL YOUR PLANS FAIL...
WHAT DO YOU MEAN?
THERE'LL BE HUNDREDS OF GUARDS AND YOU WANT TO TACKLE THEM ALL?
WHAT'RE YOU, A SCAREDY-CAT?
NO, I JUST THINK WE COULD USE A BETTER PLAN!
WELL, UNCLE, IT WON'T BE A PROBLEM FOR YOU AND TRAP TO GET IN: YOU'RE MUSKETEERS!
BUT HOW'RE WE SUPPOSED TO GET IN? WE'RE DRESSED LIKE BANDITS!
HMMM...
WHAT IS IT?

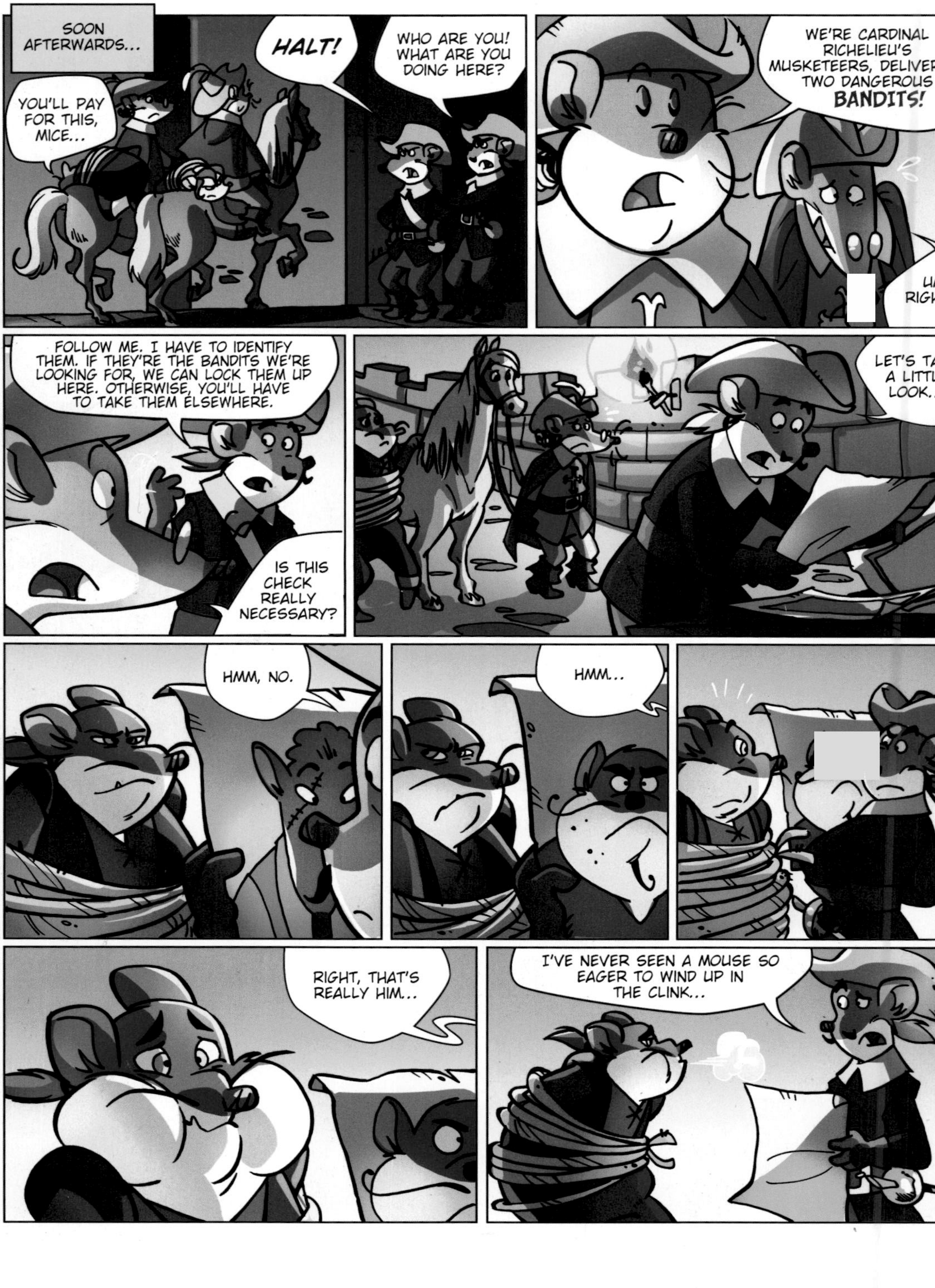
SOON AFTERWARDS...
HALT!
WHO ARE YOU! WHAT ARE YOU DOING HERE?
YOU'LL PAY FOR THIS, MICE...
WE'RE CARDINAL RICHELIEU'S MUSKETEERS, DELIVERING TWO DANGEROUS BANDITS!
UM, RIGHT...
FOLLOW ME. I HAVE TO IDENTIFY THEM. IF THEY'RE THE BANDITS WE'RE LOOKING FOR, WE CAN LOCK THEM UP HERE. OTHERWISE, YOU'LL HAVE TO TAKE THEM ELSEWHERE.
IS THIS CHECK REALLY NECESSARY?
LET'S TAKE A LITTLE LOOK...
HMM, NO.
HMM...
RIGHT, THAT'S REALLY HIM...
I'VE NEVER SEEN A MOUSE SO EAGER TO WIND UP IN THE CLINK...

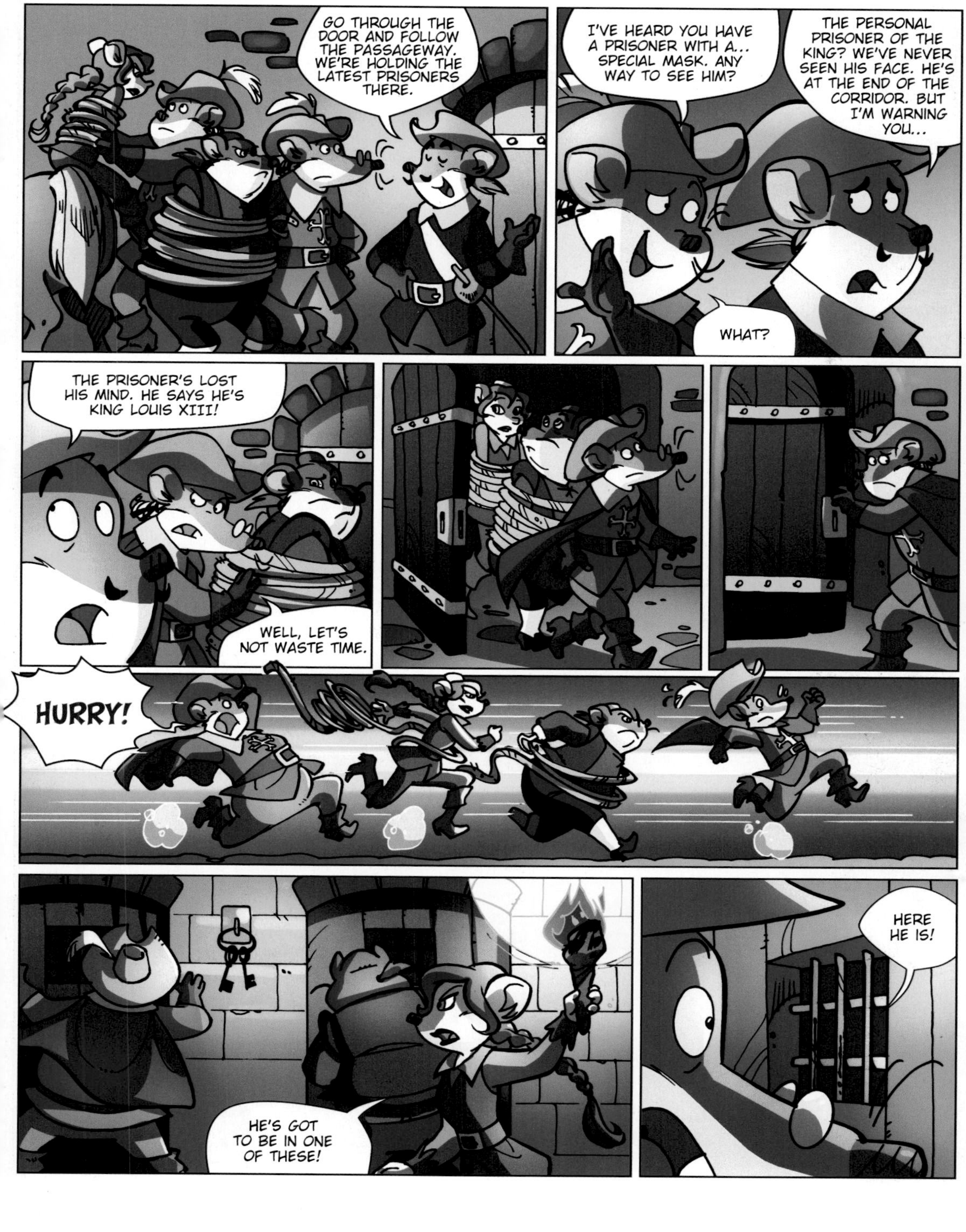
GO THROUGH THE DOOR AND FOLLOW THE PASSAGEWAY. WE'RE HOLDING THE LATEST PRISONERS THERE.
I'VE HEARD YOU HAVE A PRISONER WITH A... SPECIAL MASK. ANY WAY TO SEE HIM?
THE PERSONAL PRISONER OF THE KING? WE'VE NEVER SEEN HIS FACE. HE'S AT THE END OF THE CORRIDOR. BUT I'M WARNING YOU...
WHAT?
THE PRISONER'S LOST HIS MIND. HE SAYS HE'S KING LOUIS XIII!
WELL, LET'S NOT WASTE TIME.
HURRY!
HE'S GOT TO BE IN ONE OF THESE!
HERE HE IS!

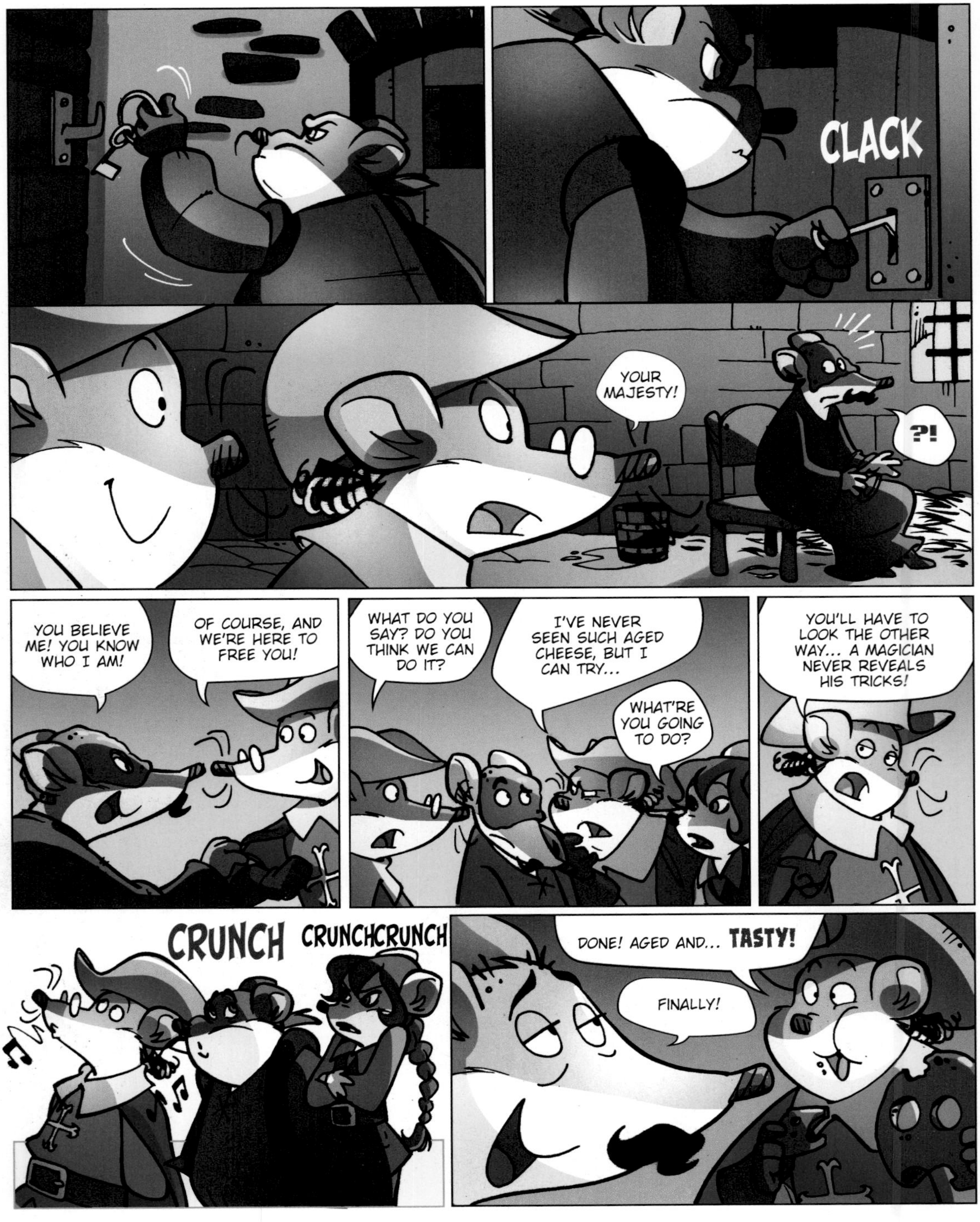
CLACK
YOUR MAJESTY!
?!
YOU BELIEVE ME! YOU KNOW WHO I AM!
OF COURSE, AND WE'RE HERE TO FREE YOU!
WHAT DO YOU SAY? DO YOU THINK WE CAN DO IT?
I'VE NEVER SEEN SUCH AGED CHEESE, BUT I CAN TRY...
WHAT'RE YOU GOING TO DO?
YOU'LL HAVE TO LOOK THE OTHER WAY... A MAGICIAN NEVER REVEALS HIS TRICKS!
CRUNCH
CRUNCHCRUNCH
DONE! AGED AND... TASTY!
FINALLY!

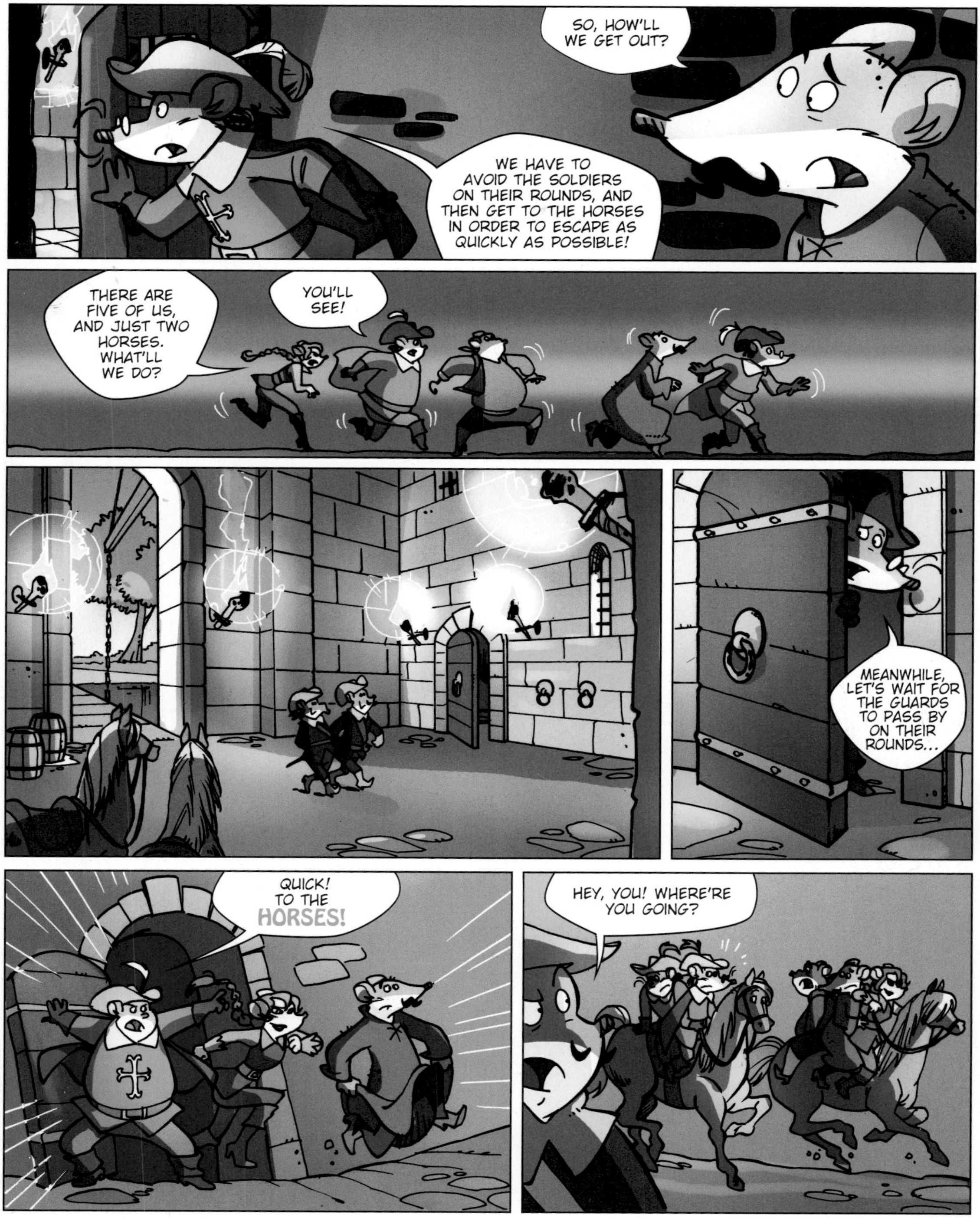

SO, HOW'LL WE GET OUT?
WE HAVE TO AVOID THE SOLDIERS ON THEIR ROUNDS, AND THEN GET TO THE HORSES IN ORDER TO ESCAPE AS QUICKLY AS POSSIBLE!
THERE ARE FIVE OF US, AND JUST TWO HORSES. WHAT'LL WE DO?
YOU'LL SEE!
MEANWHILE, LET'S WAIT FOR THE GUARDS TO PASS BY ON THEIR ROUNDS...
QUICK! TO THE HORSES!
HEY, YOU! WHERE'RE YOU GOING?

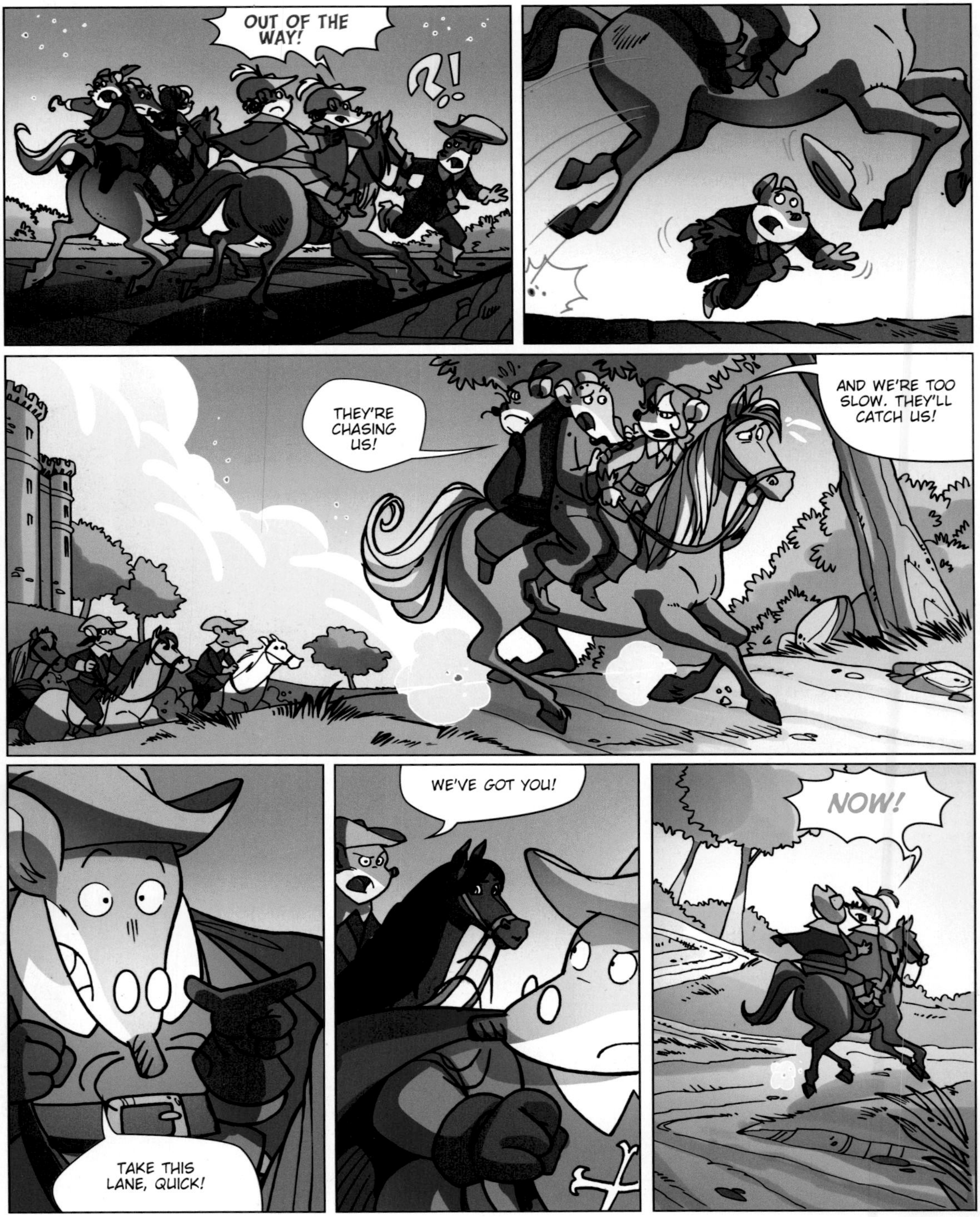
OUT OF THE WAY!
?!
THEY'RE CHASING US!
AND WE'RE TOO SLOW. THEY'LL CATCH US!
TAKE THIS LANE, QUICK!
WE'VE GOT YOU!
NOW!

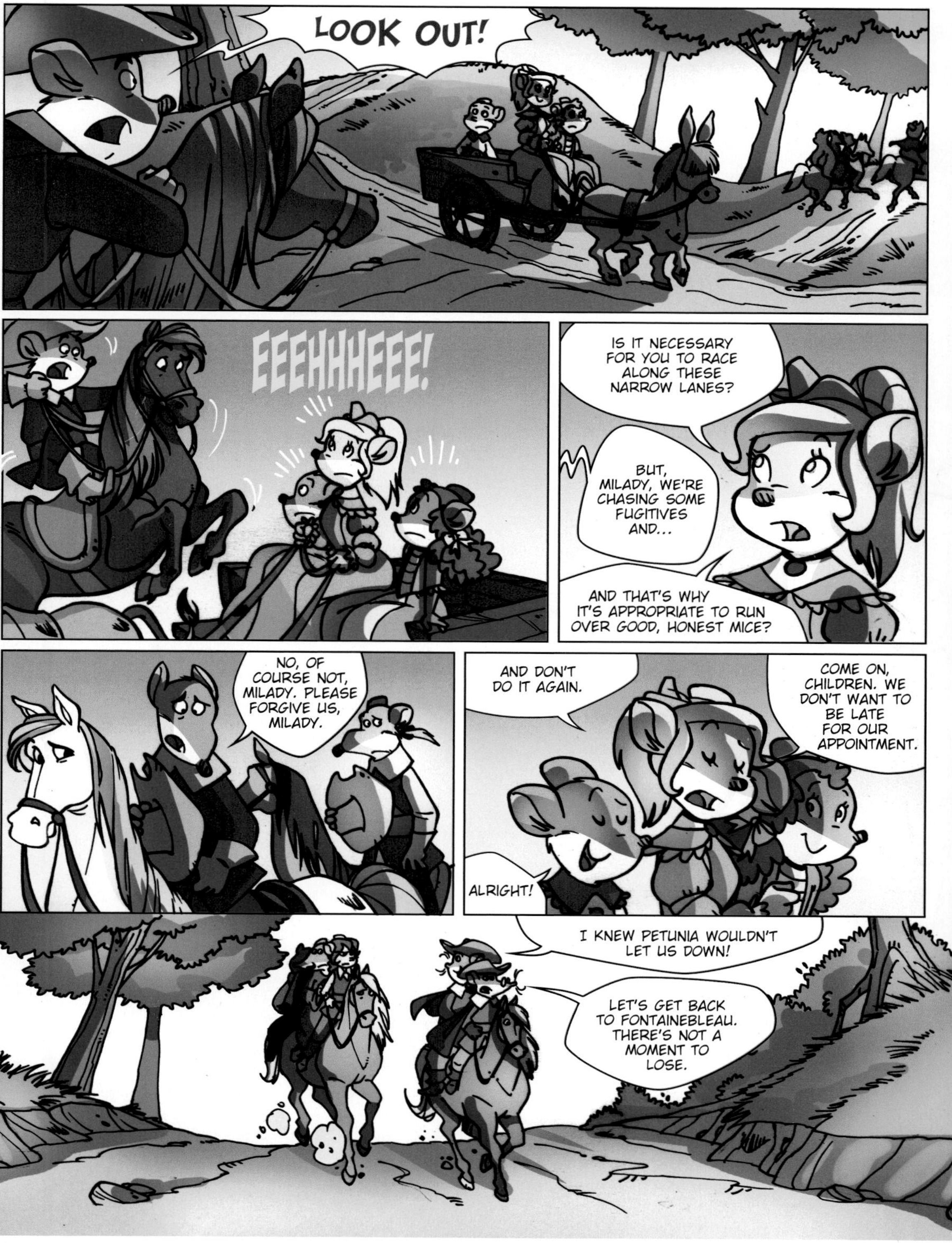
LOOK OUT!
EEEHHHEEE!
IS IT NECESSARY FOR YOU TO RACE ALONG THESE NARROW LANES?
BUT, MILADY, WE'RE CHASING SOME FUGITIVES AND...
AND THAT'S WHY IT'S APPROPRIATE TO RUN OVER GOOD, HONEST MICE?
NO, OF COURSE NOT, MILADY. PLEASE FORGIVE US, MILADY.
AND DON'T DO IT AGAIN.
COME ON, CHILDREN. WE DON'T WANT TO BE LATE FOR OUR APPOINTMENT.
ALRIGHT!
I KNEW PETUNIA WOULDN'T LET US DOWN!
LET'S GET BACK TO FONTAINEBLEAU. THERE'S NOT A MOMENT TO LOSE.

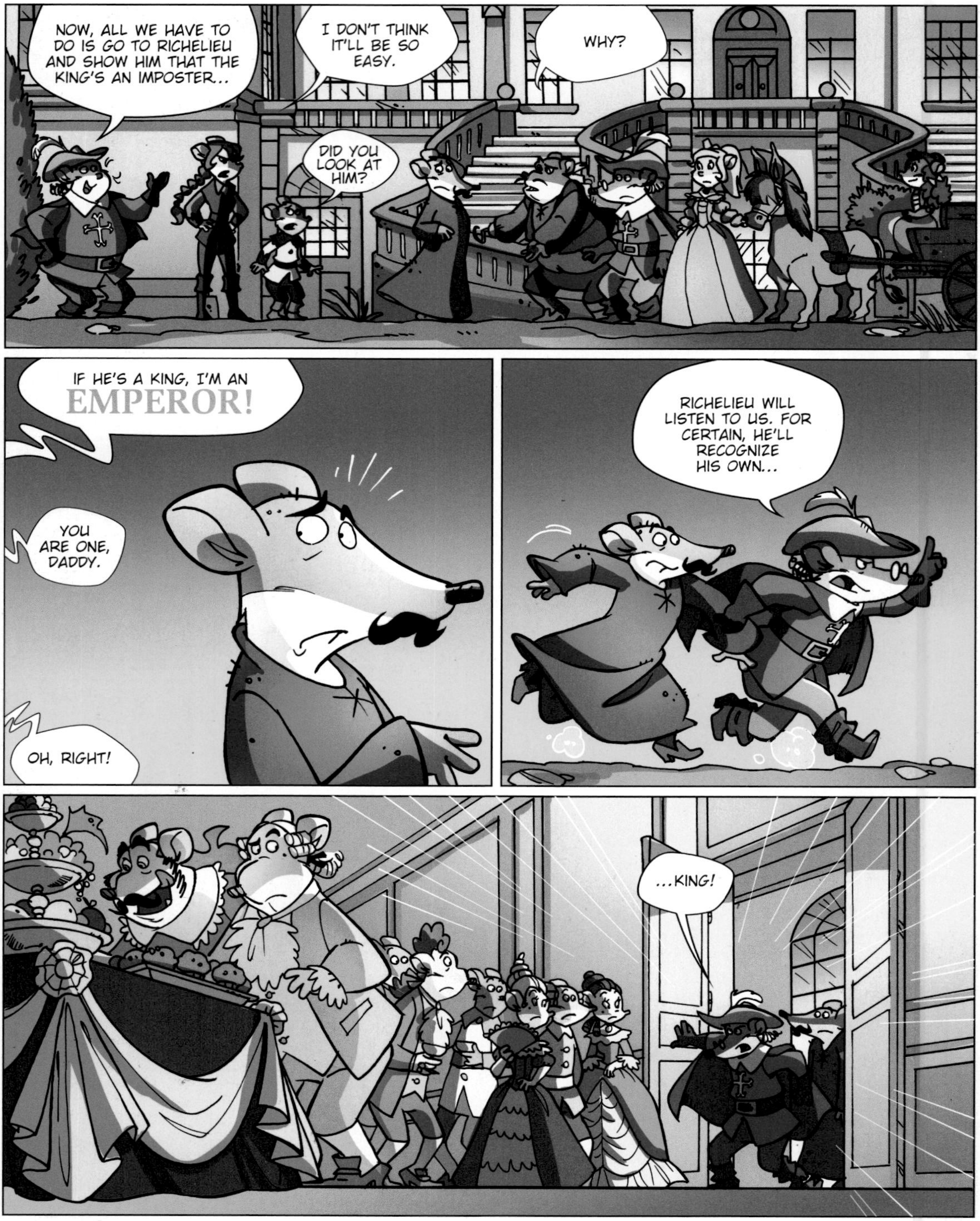
NOW, ALL WE HAVE TO DO IS GO TO RICHELIEU AND SHOW HIM THAT THE KING'S AN IMPOSTER...
I DON'T THINK IT'LL BE SO EASY.
WHY?
DID YOU LOOK AT HIM?
IF HE'S A KING, I'M AN EMPEROR!
YOU ARE ONE, DADDY.
OH, RIGHT!
RICHELIEU WILL LISTEN TO US. FOR CERTAIN, HE'LL RECOGNIZE HIS OWN...
...KING!

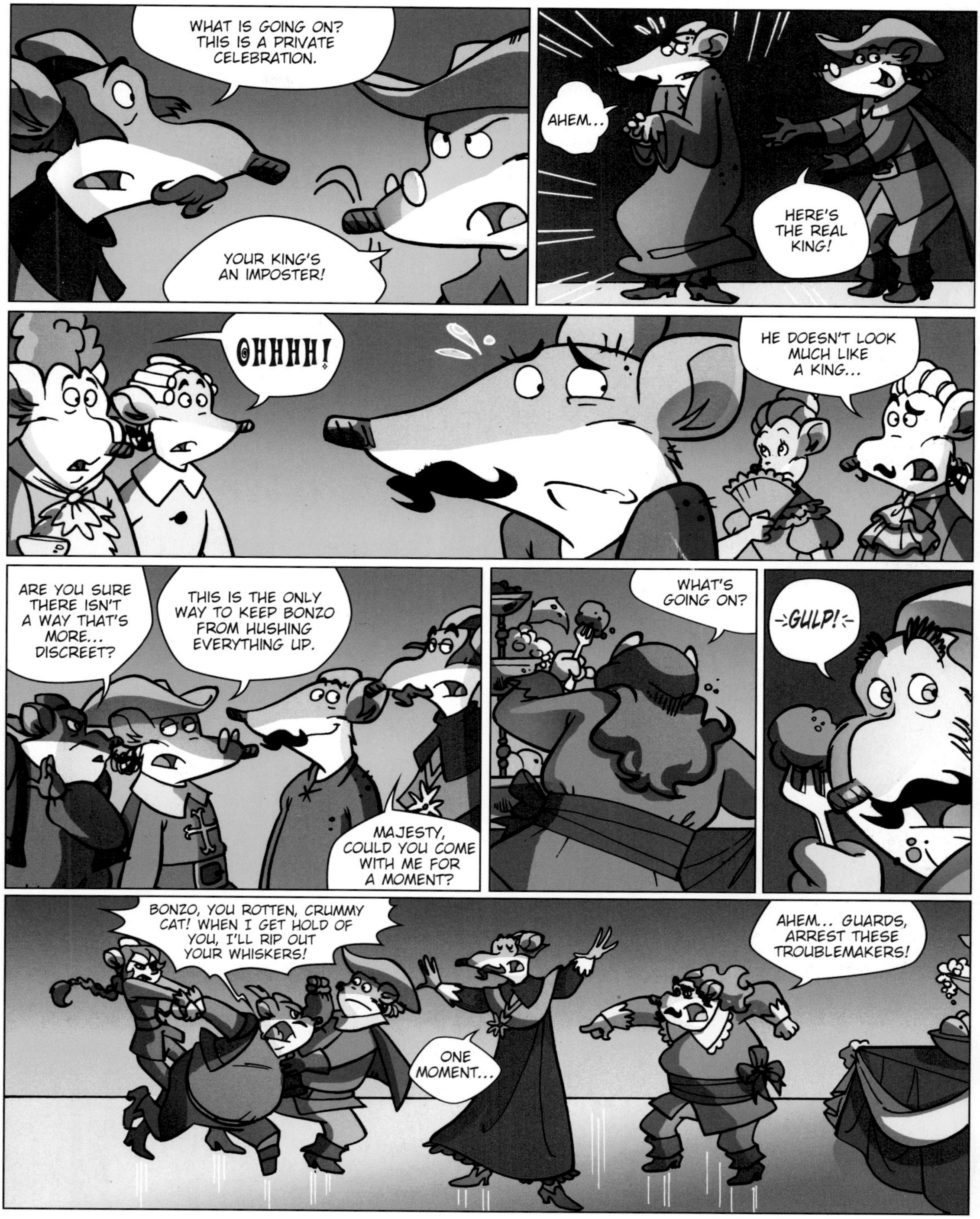

WHAT IS GOING ON? THIS IS A PRIVATE CELEBRATION.
YOUR KING'S AN IMPOSTER!
AHEM...
HERE'S THE REAL KING!
OHHHH!
HE DOESN'T LOOK MUCH LIKE A KING...
ARE YOU SURE THERE ISN'T A WAY THAT'S MORE... DISCREET?
THIS IS THE ONLY WAY TO KEEP BONZO FROM HUSHING EVERYTHING UP.
MAJESTY, COULD YOU COME WITH ME FOR A MOMENT?
WHAT'S GOING ON?
GULP!
BONZO, YOU ROTTEN, CRUMMY CAT! WHEN I GET HOLD OF YOU, I'LL RIP OUT YOUR WHISKERS!
ONE MOMENT...
AHEM... GUARDS, ARREST THESE TROUBLEMAKERS!

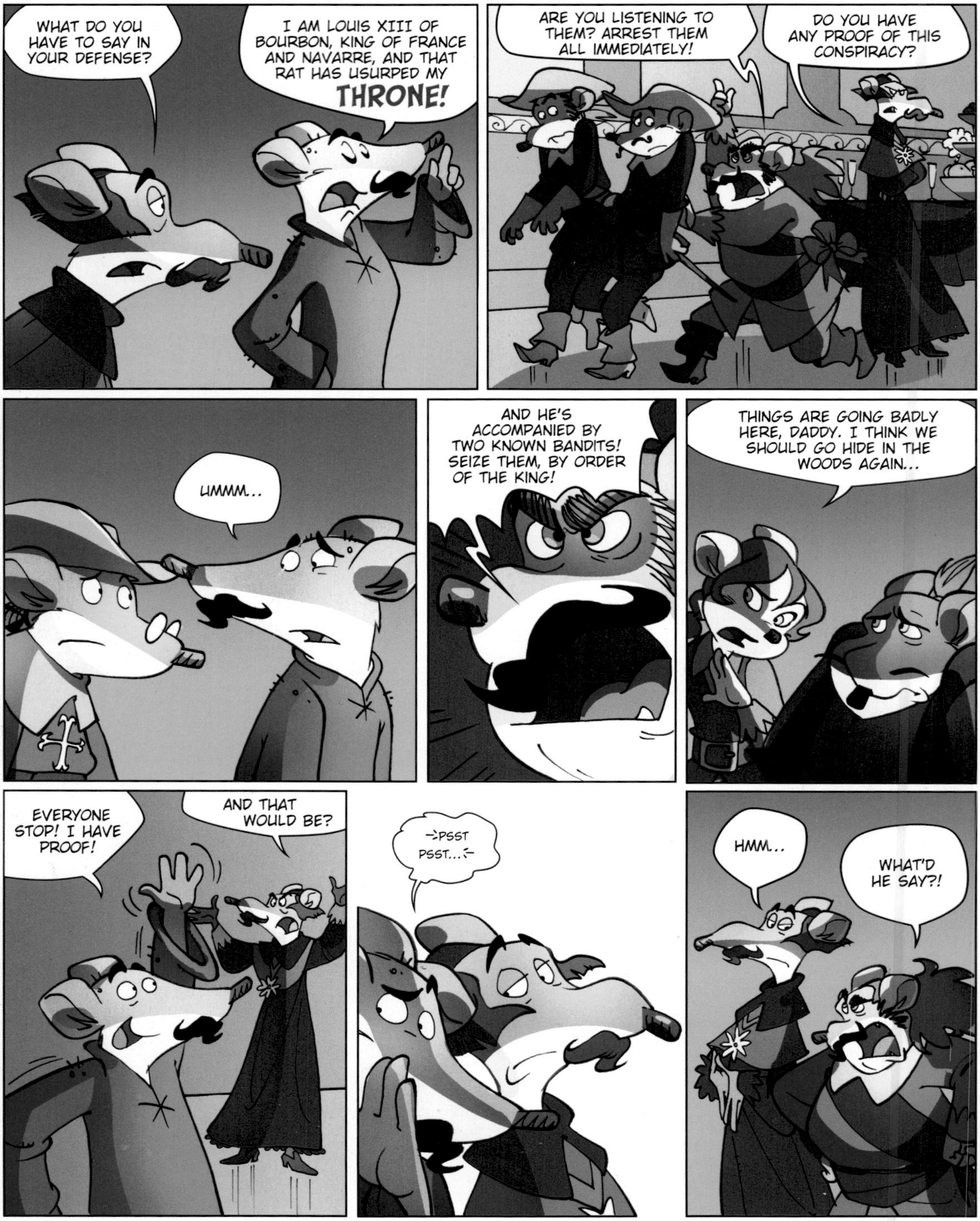
WHAT DO YOU HAVE TO SAY IN YOUR DEFENSE?
I AM LOUIS XIII OF BOURBON, KING OF FRANCE AND NAVARRE, AND THAT RAT HAS USURPED MY THRONE!
ARE YOU LISTENING TO THEM? ARREST THEM ALL IMMEDIATELY!
DO YOU HAVE ANY PROOF OF THIS CONSPIRACY?
UMMM...
AND HE'S ACCOMPANIED BY TWO KNOWN BANDITS! SEIZE THEM, BY ORDER OF THE KING!
THINGS ARE GOING BADLY HERE, DADDY. I THINK WE SHOULD GO HIDE IN THE WOODS AGAIN...
EVERYONE STOP! I HAVE PROOF!
AND THAT WOULD BE?
PSST PSST...
HMM...
WHAT'D HE SAY?!

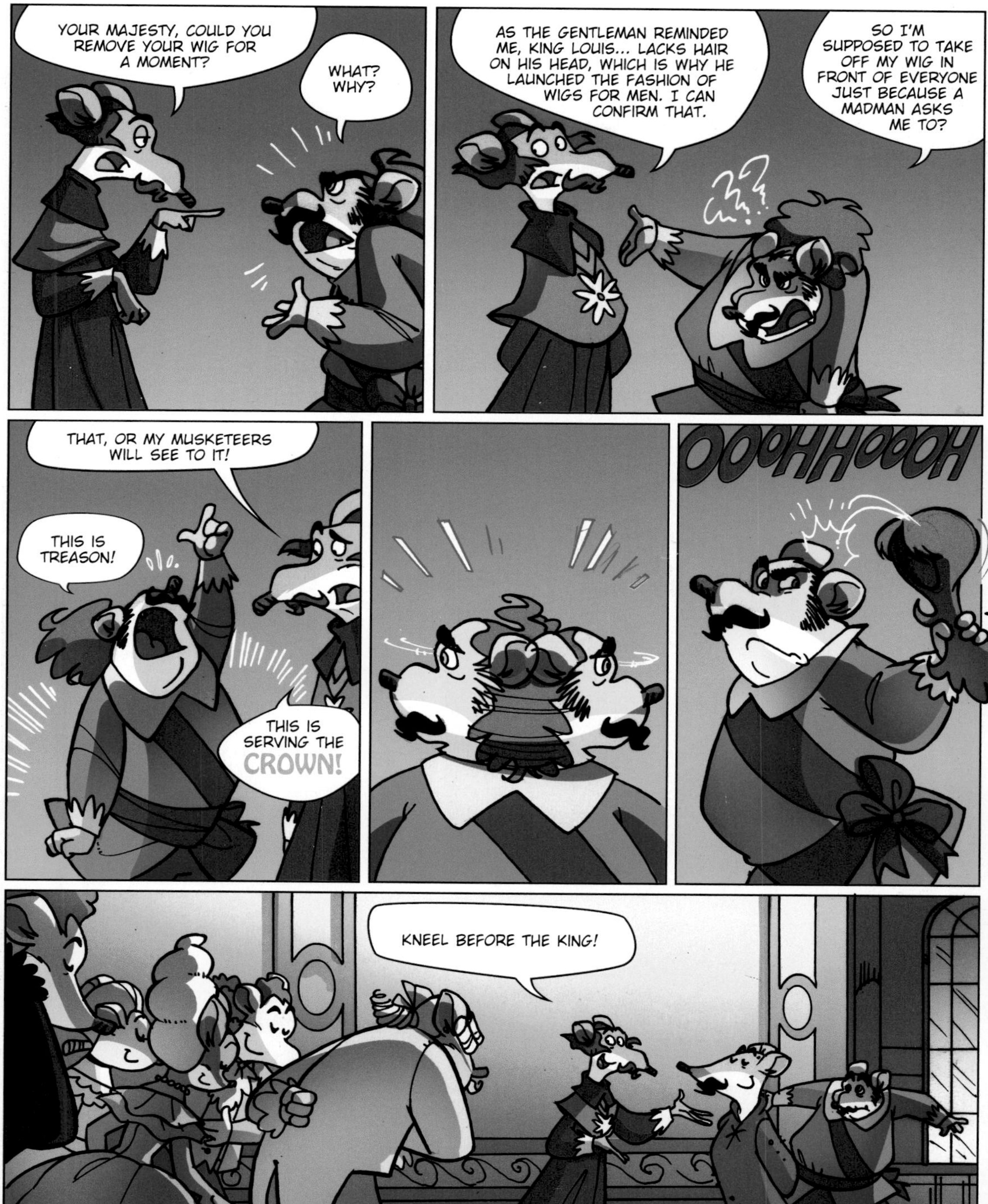
YOUR MAJESTY, COULD YOU REMOVE YOUR WIG FOR A MOMENT?
WHAT? WHY?
AS THE GENTLEMAN REMINDED ME, KING LOUIS... LACKS HAIR ON HIS HEAD, WHICH IS WHY HE LAUNCHED THE FASHION OF WIGS FOR MEN. I CAN CONFIRM THAT.
SO I'M SUPPOSED TO TAKE OFF MY WIG IN FRONT OF EVERYONE JUST BECAUSE A MADMAN ASKS ME TO?
THAT, OR MY MUSKETEERS WILL SEE TO IT!
THIS IS TREASON!
THIS IS SERVING THE CROWN!
OOOHHOOOH
KNEEL BEFORE THE KING!

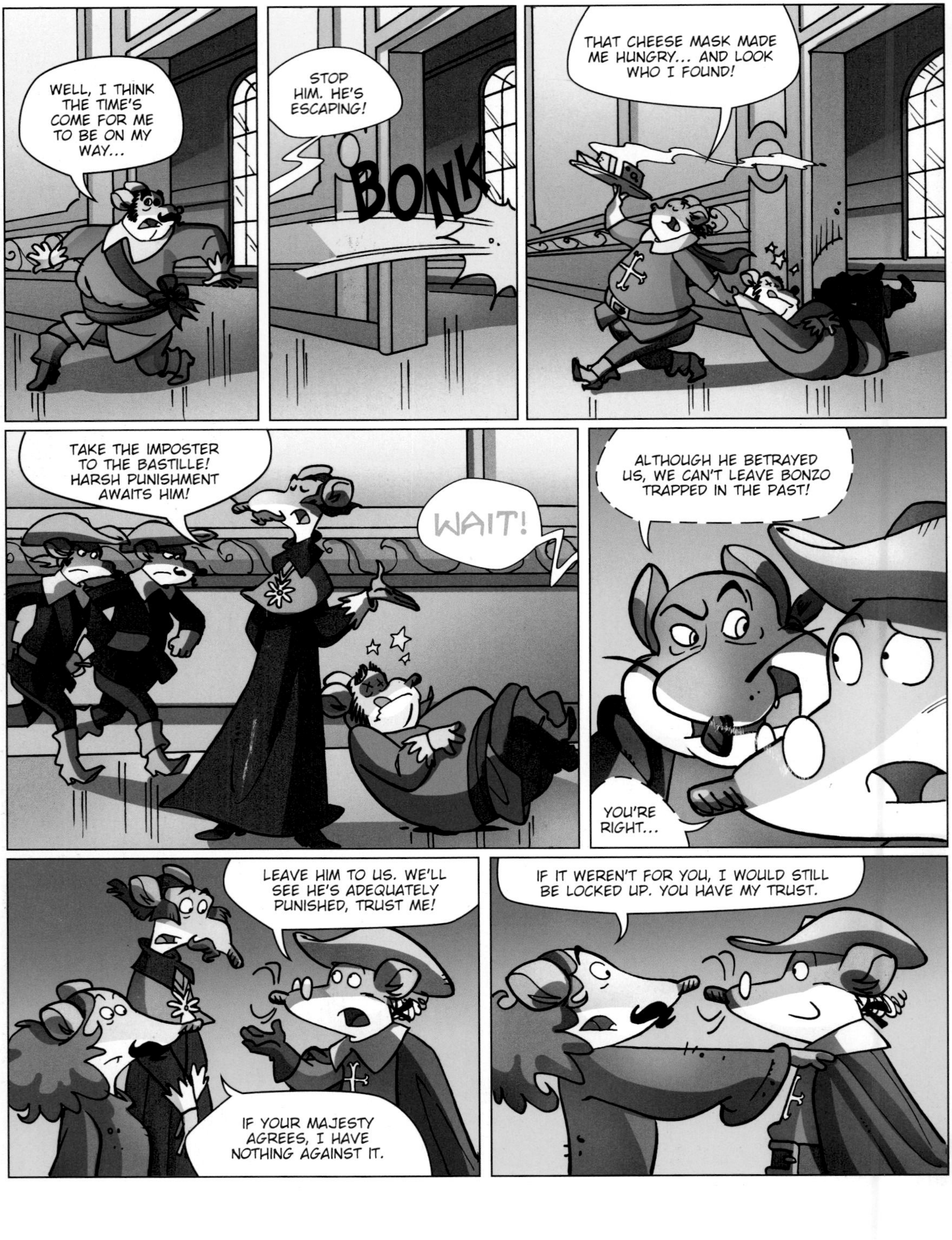
WELL, I THINK THE TIME'S COME FOR ME TO BE ON MY WAY...
STOP HIM. HE'S ESCAPING!
BONK
THAT CHEESE MASK MADE ME HUNGRY... AND LOOK WHO I FOUND!
TAKE THE IMPOSTER TO THE BASTILLE! HARSH PUNISHMENT AWAITS HIM!
WAIT!
ALTHOUGH HE BETRAYED US, WE CAN'T LEAVE BONZO TRAPPED IN THE PAST!
YOU'RE RIGHT...
LEAVE HIM TO US. WE'LL SEE HE'S ADEQUATELY PUNISHED, TRUST ME!
IF YOUR MAJESTY AGREES, I HAVE NOTHING AGAINST IT.
IF IT WEREN'T FOR YOU, I WOULD STILL BE LOCKED UP. YOU HAVE MY TRUST.

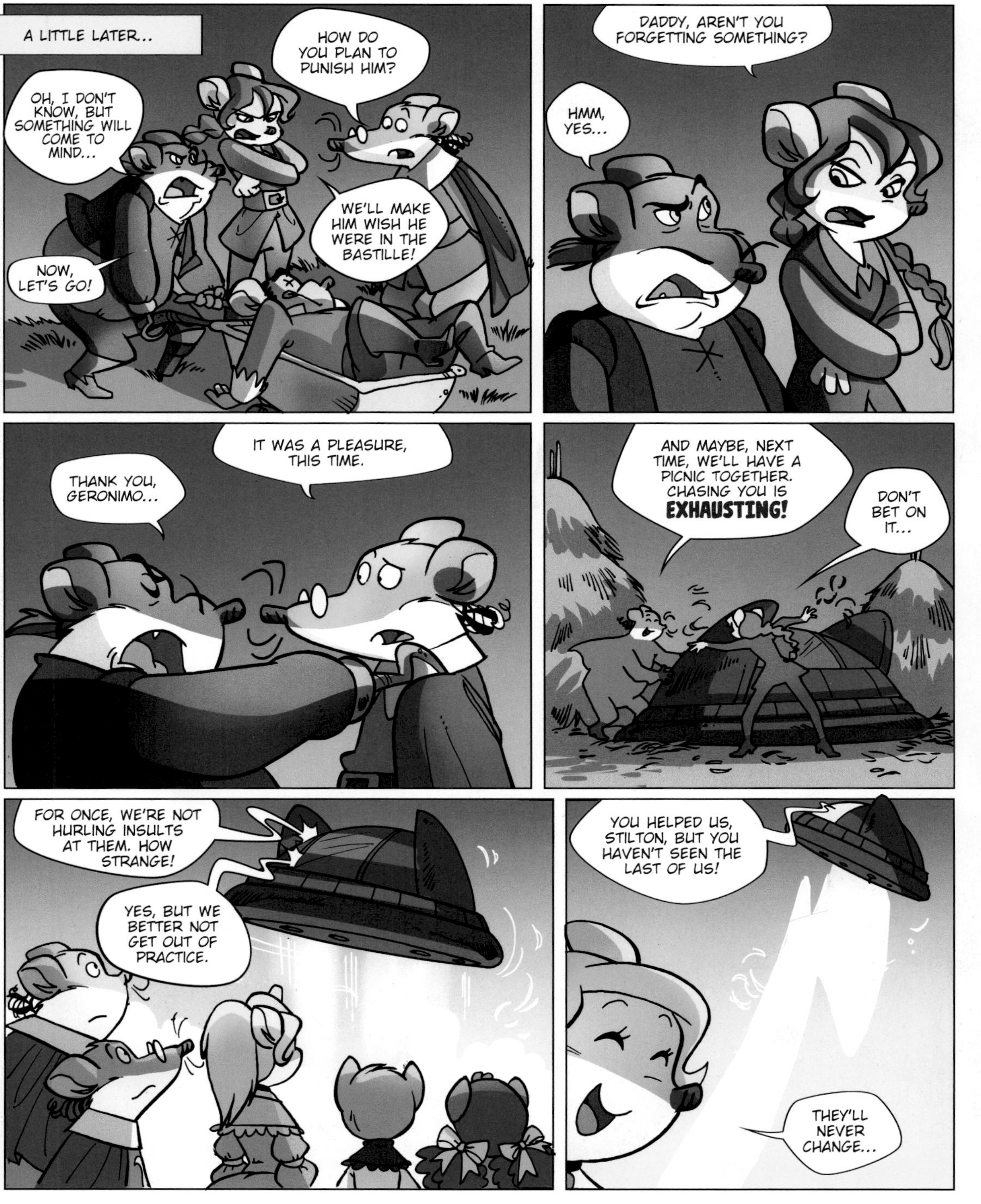
A LITTLE LATER...
HOW DO YOU PLAN TO PUNISH HIM?
OH, I DON'T KNOW, BUT SOMETHING WILL COME TO MIND...
WE'LL MAKE HIM WISH HE WERE IN THE BASTILLE!
NOW, LET'S GO!
DADDY, AREN'T YOU FORGETTING SOMETHING?
HMM, YES...
THANK YOU, GERONIMO...
IT WAS A PLEASURE, THIS TIME.
AND MAYBE, NEXT TIME, WE'LL HAVE A PICNIC TOGETHER. CHASING YOU IS **EXHAUSTING!**
DON'T BET ON IT...
FOR ONCE, WE'RE NOT HURLING INSULTS AT THEM. HOW STRANGE!
YES, BUT WE BETTER NOT GET OUT OF PRACTICE.
YOU HELPED US, STILTON, BUT YOU HAVEN'T SEEN THE LAST OF US!
THEY'LL NEVER CHANGE...

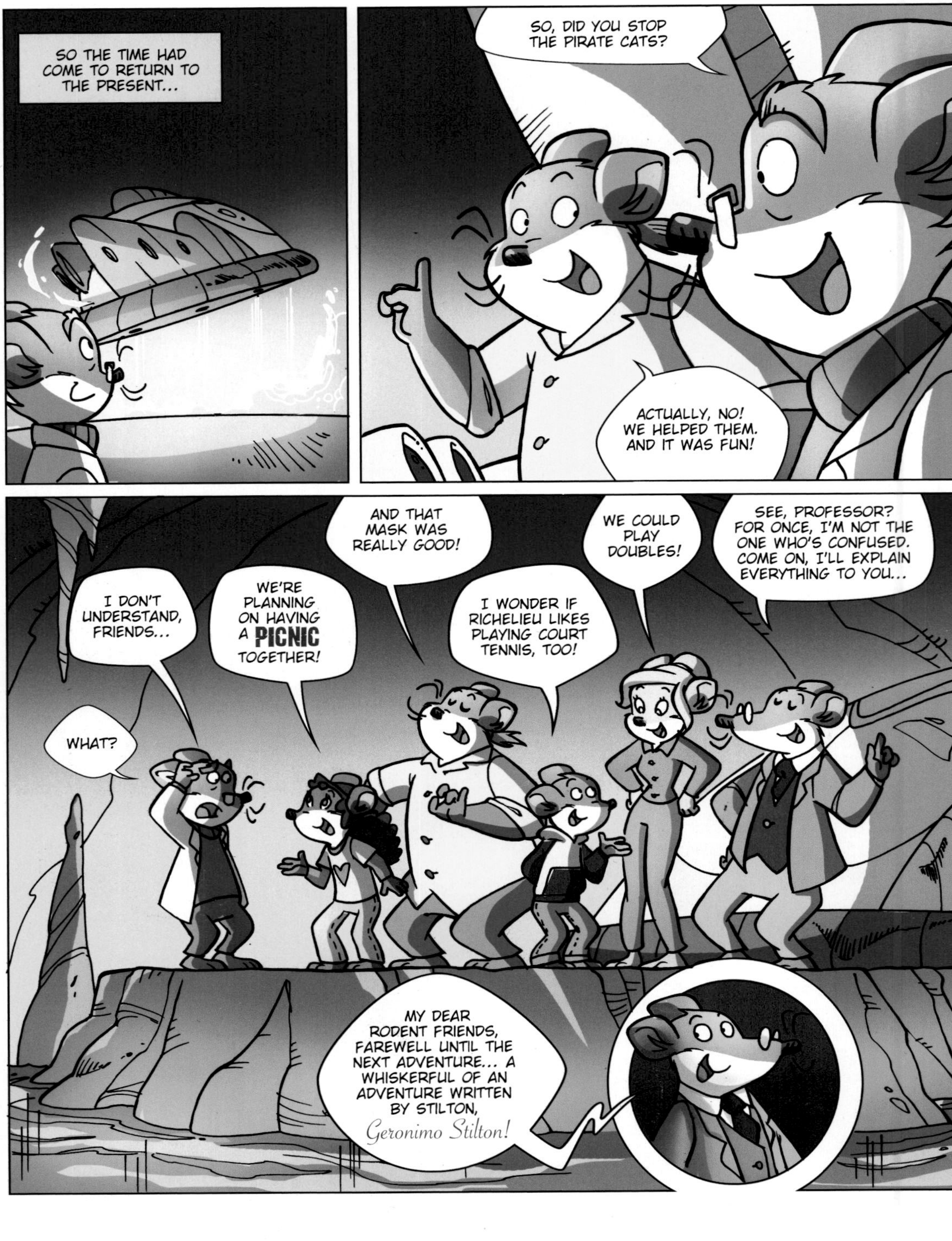
SO THE TIME HAD COME TO RETURN TO THE PRESENT...
SO, DID YOU STOP THE PIRATE CATS?
ACTUALLY, NO! WE HELPED THEM. AND IT WAS FUN!
I DON'T UNDERSTAND, FRIENDS...
WHAT?
WE'RE PLANNING ON HAVING A PICNIC TOGETHER!
AND THAT MASK WAS REALLY GOOD!
I WONDER IF RICHELIEU LIKES PLAYING COURT TENNIS, TOO!
WE COULD PLAY DOUBLES!
SEE, PROFESSOR? FOR ONCE, I'M NOT THE ONE WHO'S CONFUSED. COME ON, I'LL EXPLAIN EVERYTHING TO YOU...
MY DEAR RODENT FRIENDS, FAREWELL UNTIL THE NEXT ADVENTURE... A WHISKERFUL OF AN ADVENTURE WRITTEN BY STILTON, Geronimo Stilton!

Watch Out For PAPERCUTZ™

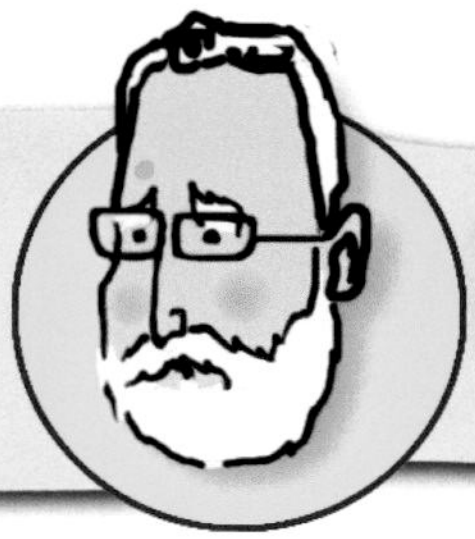

Welcome to the French-flavored, fifteenth GERONIMO STILTON graphic novel from Papercutz, those fencing-class failures dedicated to publishing great graphic novels for all ages. I'm Salicrup, *Jim Salicrup*, the Editor-in-Chief and honorary Mouseketeer (I even appeared on The New Mickey Mouse Club TV series!). I'm here to provide a little background to further your enjoyment of GERONIMO STILTON.

If you're a fan of classic adventure fiction, then you probably enjoyed the various references to *The Three Musketeers* throughout this Geronimo Stilton graphic novel. But whether you've read the original novel by Alexandre Dumas or not, we're sure you'll enjoy the adaptation of "The Three Musketeers," written by Jean David Morvan and Michel Dufranne, and illustrated by Rubén, that we published in CLASSICS ILLUSTRATED DELUXE #6. And if you're not familiar with CLASSICS ILLUSTRATED, well…

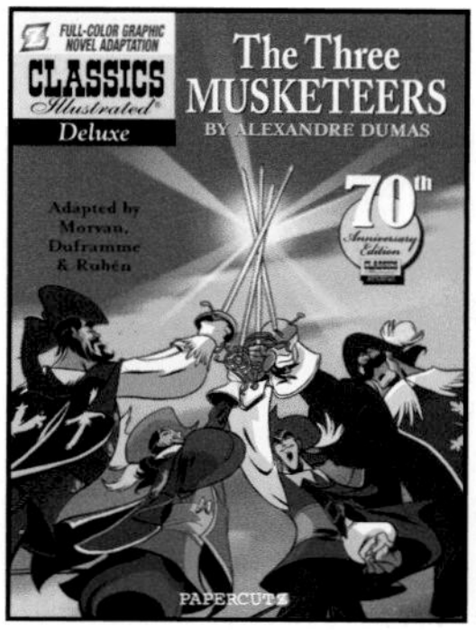

FULL-COLOR GRAPHIC NOVEL ADAPTATION
CLASSICS Illustrated Deluxe
The Three MUSKETEERS
BY ALEXANDRE DUMAS
Adapted by Morvan, Dufranne & Rubén
70th Anniversary Edition
PAPERCUTZ

As William B. Jones Jr. wrote in CLASSICS ILLUSTRATED #1 "Great Expectations," "CLASSICS ILLUSTRATED was the brainchild of Albert Lewis Kanter, a visionary publisher, who deserves to be ranked among the great teachers of the 20th century. From 1941 to 1971, he introduced young readers to the realms of literature, history, folklore, mythology, and science in such comicbook juvenile series as CLASSICS ILLUSTRATED, CLASSICS ILLUSTRATED JUNIOR, CLASSICS ILLUSTRATED SPECIAL SERIES, and THE WORLD AROUND US."

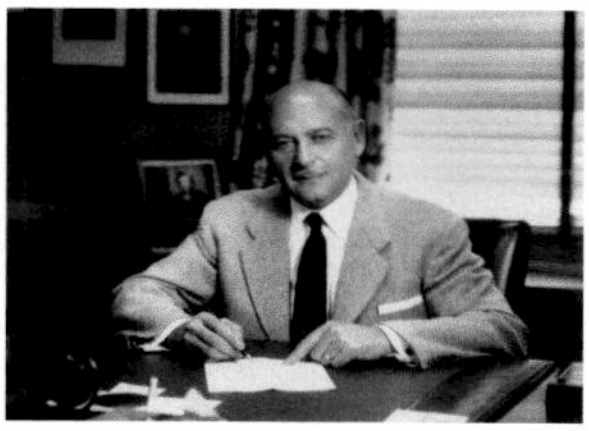

Photo of Albert Kanter courtesy of Hal Kanter.

When comicbooks, filled with the adventures of larger-than-life super-heroes, were taking America's youth by storm back in the early 40s "Kanter believed he could use the same medium to introduce young readers to the world of great literature." Or as Geronimo Stilton would say, great liteRATure! In October 1941, "with the backing of two business partners, Kanter launched CLASSICS COMICS [the title was later changed to CLASSICS ILLUSTRATED]." And guess what was the very first classic they adapted into comics form? That's right! *The Three Musketeers!* To compete with the likes of Superman and Captain America, Kanter brought the great literary heroes to comicbook life.

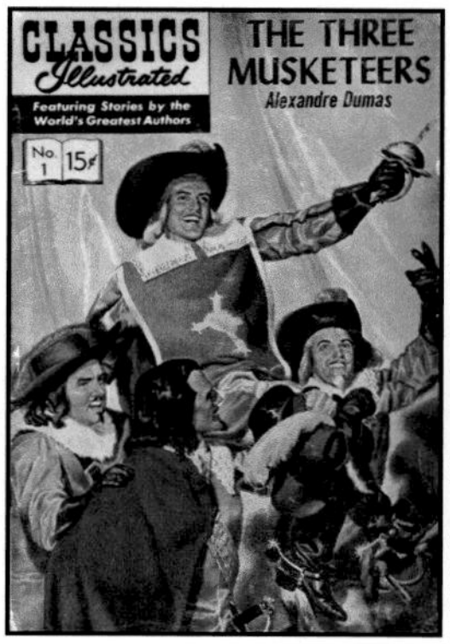

CLASSICS Illustrated
Featuring Stories by the World's Greatest Authors
THE THREE MUSKETEERS
Alexandre Dumas
No. 1 15¢

While that comics adaptation is still available digitally and in print, there aren't that many of CLASSICS ILLUSTRATED DELUXE #6 still in print. We're currently sold out, but if you check your favorite online bookseller, you may still be able to get a copy. Of course, you can always get the original novel, available at booksellers everywhere, as well as at your school or library. Fortunately, the GERONIMO STILTON graphic novel you have right now, gives you a taste of the adventure that awaits you in the Dumas classic!

Of course, you won't want to miss the next exciting Geronimo Stilton adventure either! On the following pages is a preview of GERONIMO STILTON #16 "Lights, Camera, Stilton!" Once again our favorite Editor of *The Rodent's Gazette* must save the future, by protecting the past!

See you in the future!

JIM

STAY IN TOUCH!

EMAIL: salicrup@papercutz.com
WEB: papercutz.com
TWITTER: @papercutzgn
FACEBOOK: PAPERCUTZGRAPHICNOVELS
FAN MAIL: Papercutz, 160 Broadway, Suite 700, East Wing, New York, NY 10038

Special preview of GERONIMO STILTON #16 “ Lights, Camera, Stilton!”

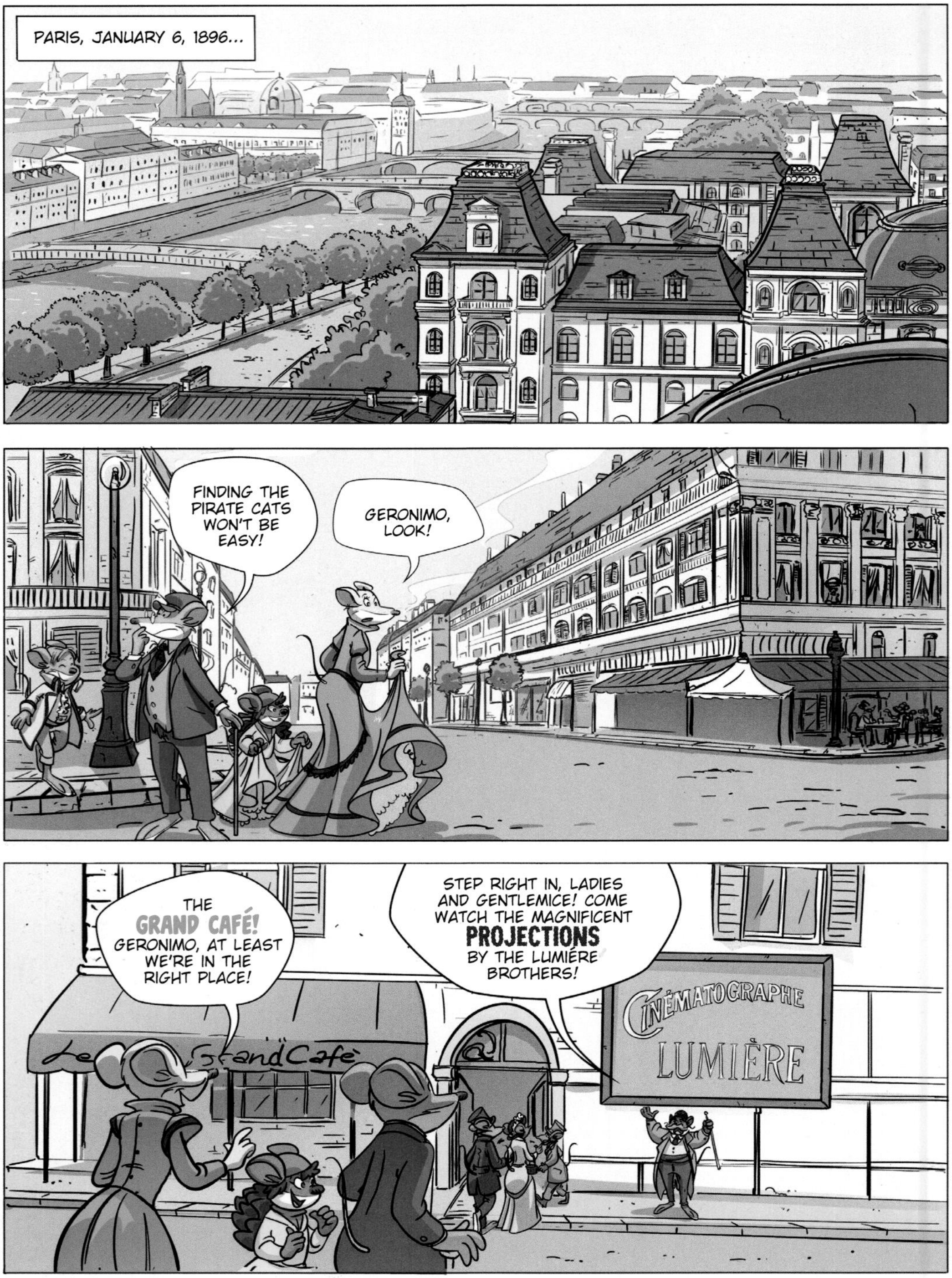
PARIS, JANUARY 6, 1896...
FINDING THE PIRATE CATS WON'T BE EASY!
GERONIMO, LOOK!
THE GRAND CAFÉ! GERONIMO, AT LEAST WE'RE IN THE RIGHT PLACE!
STEP RIGHT IN, LADIES AND GENTLEMICE! COME WATCH THE MAGNIFICENT PROJECTIONS BY THE LUMIÉRE BROTHERS!
CINÉMATOGRAPHE
LUMIÈRE

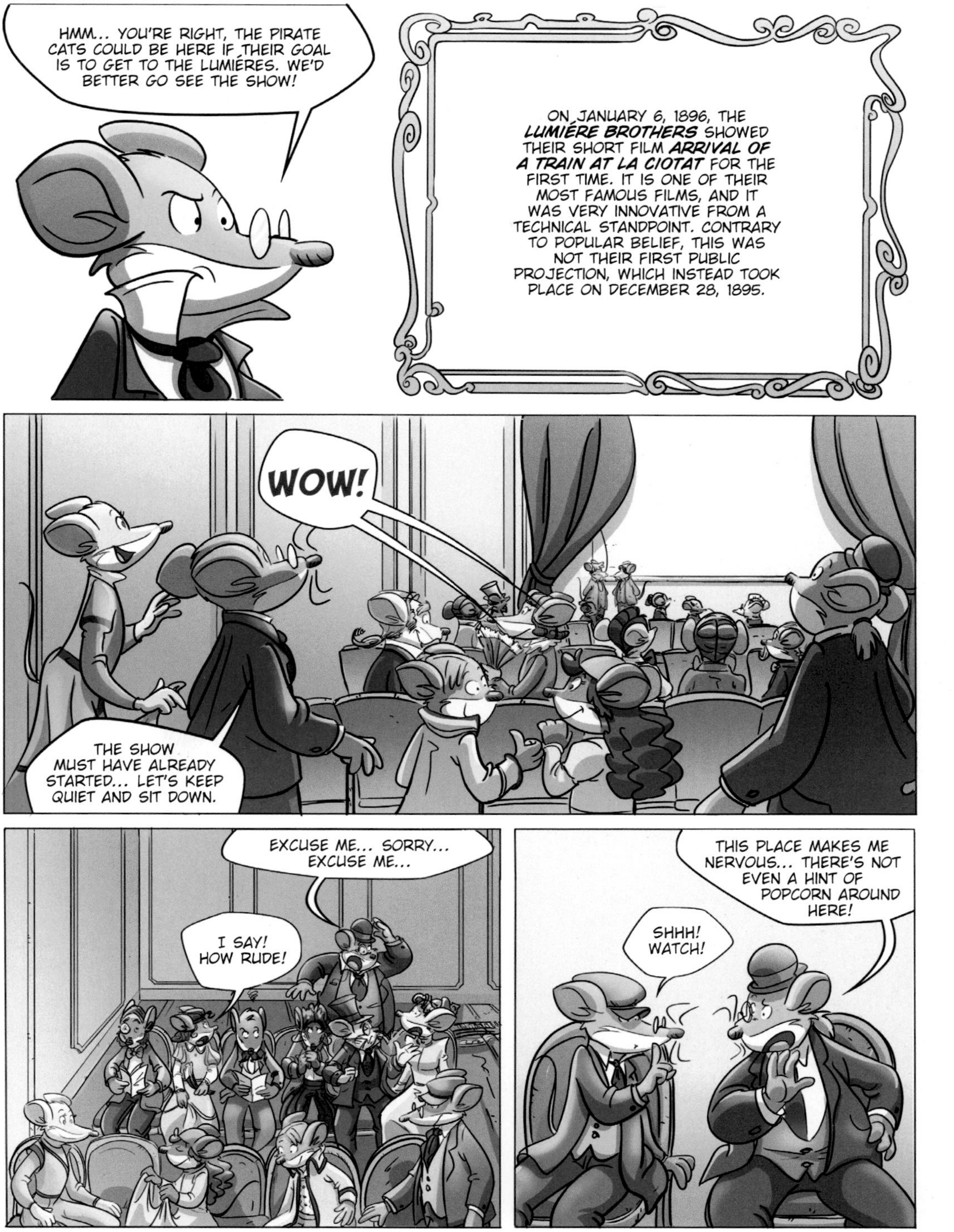

HMM... YOU'RE RIGHT, THE PIRATE CATS COULD BE HERE IF THEIR GOAL IS TO GET TO THE LUMIÉRES. WE'D BETTER GO SEE THE SHOW!
ON JANUARY 6, 1896, THE ***LUMIÉRE BROTHERS*** SHOWED THEIR SHORT FILM ***ARRIVAL OF A TRAIN AT LA CIOTAT*** FOR THE FIRST TIME. IT IS ONE OF THEIR MOST FAMOUS FILMS, AND IT WAS VERY INNOVATIVE FROM A TECHNICAL STANDPOINT. CONTRARY TO POPULAR BELIEF, THIS WAS NOT THEIR FIRST PUBLIC PROJECTION, WHICH INSTEAD TOOK PLACE ON DECEMBER 28, 1895.
WOW!
THE SHOW MUST HAVE ALREADY STARTED... LET'S KEEP QUIET AND SIT DOWN.
EXCUSE ME... SORRY... EXCUSE ME...
I SAY! HOW RUDE!
THIS PLACE MAKES ME NERVOUS... THERE'S NOT EVEN A HINT OF POPCORN AROUND HERE!
SHHH! WATCH!

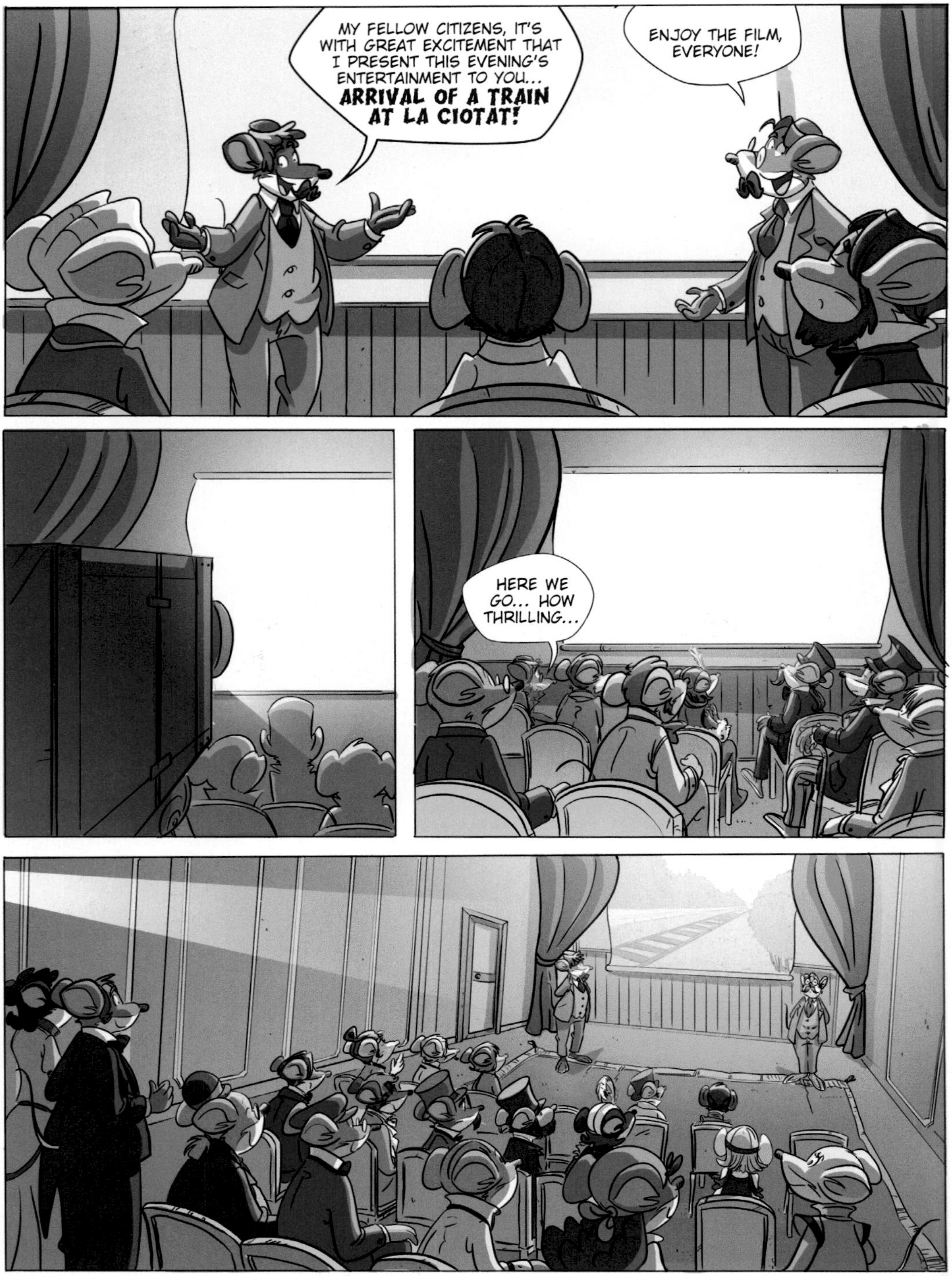
MY FELLOW CITIZENS, IT'S WITH GREAT EXCITEMENT THAT I PRESENT THIS EVENING'S ENTERTAINMENT TO YOU... **ARRIVAL OF A TRAIN AT LA CIOTAT!**
ENJOY THE FILM, EVERYONE!
HERE WE GO... HOW THRILLING...

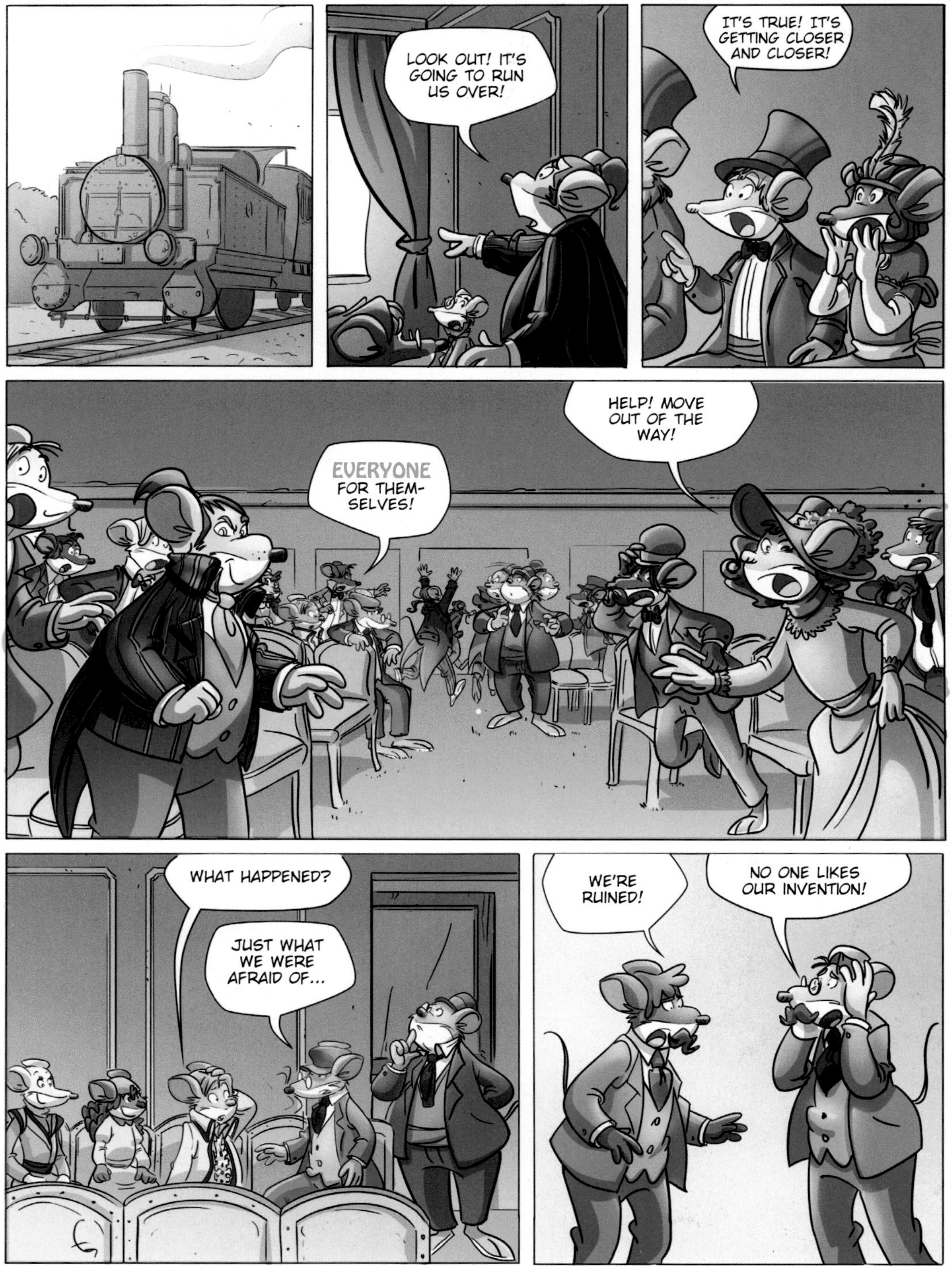
LOOK OUT! IT'S GOING TO RUN US OVER!
IT'S TRUE! IT'S GETTING CLOSER AND CLOSER!
EVERYONE FOR THEMSELVES!
HELP! MOVE OUT OF THE WAY!
WHAT HAPPENED?
JUST WHAT WE WERE AFRAID OF...
WE'RE RUINED!
NO ONE LIKES OUR INVENTION!

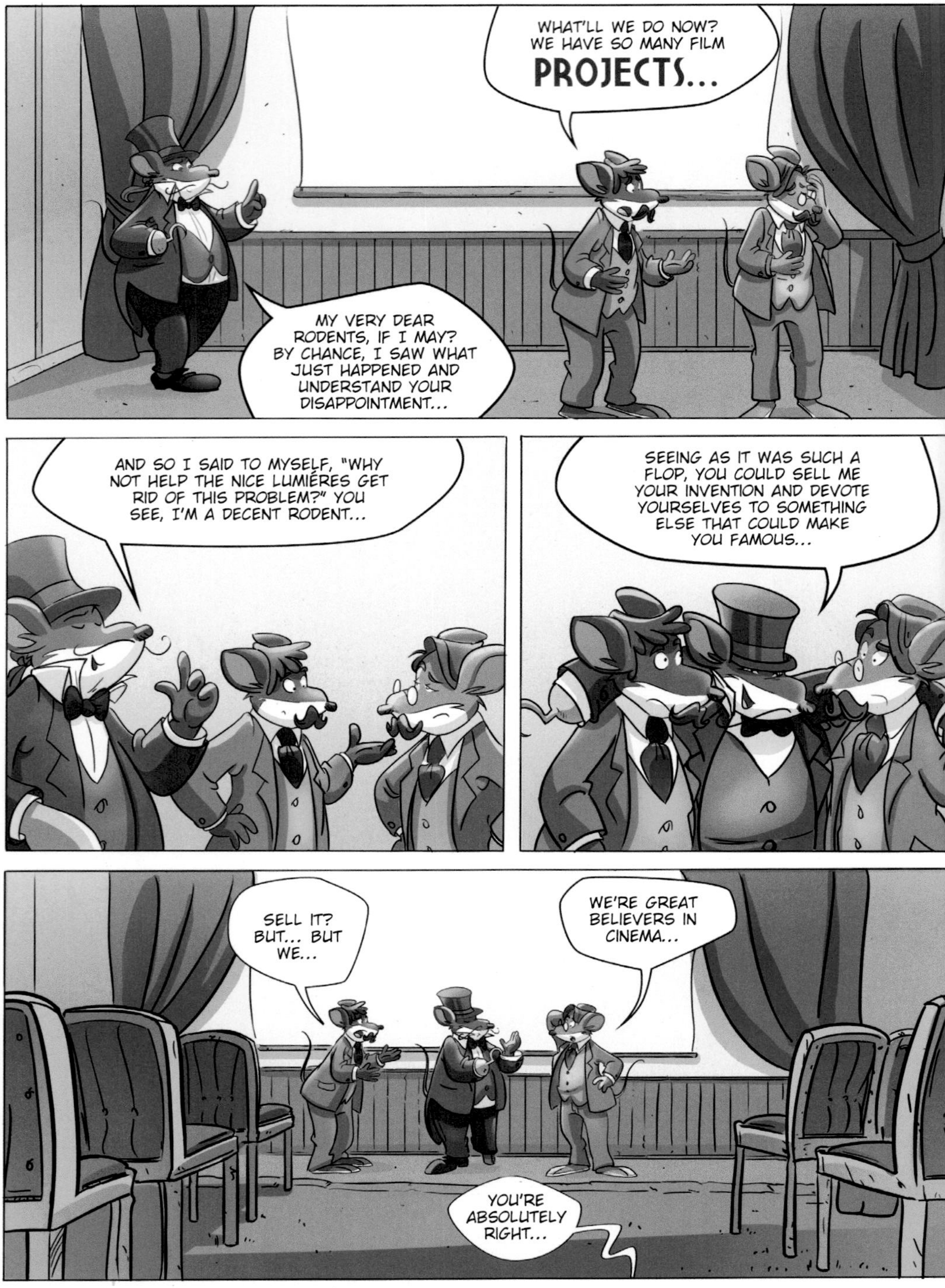

WHAT'LL WE DO NOW? WE HAVE SO MANY FILM PROJECTS...
MY VERY DEAR RODENTS, IF I MAY? BY CHANCE, I SAW WHAT JUST HAPPENED AND UNDERSTAND YOUR DISAPPOINTMENT...
AND SO I SAID TO MYSELF, "WHY NOT HELP THE NICE LUMIÉRES GET RID OF THIS PROBLEM?" YOU SEE, I'M A DECENT RODENT...
SEEING AS IT WAS SUCH A FLOP, YOU COULD SELL ME YOUR INVENTION AND DEVOTE YOURSELVES TO SOMETHING ELSE THAT COULD MAKE YOU FAMOUS...
SELL IT? BUT... BUT WE...
WE'RE GREAT BELIEVERS IN CINEMA...
YOU'RE ABSOLUTELY RIGHT...

Don't miss GERONIMO STILTON #16 "Lights, Camera, Stilton!"

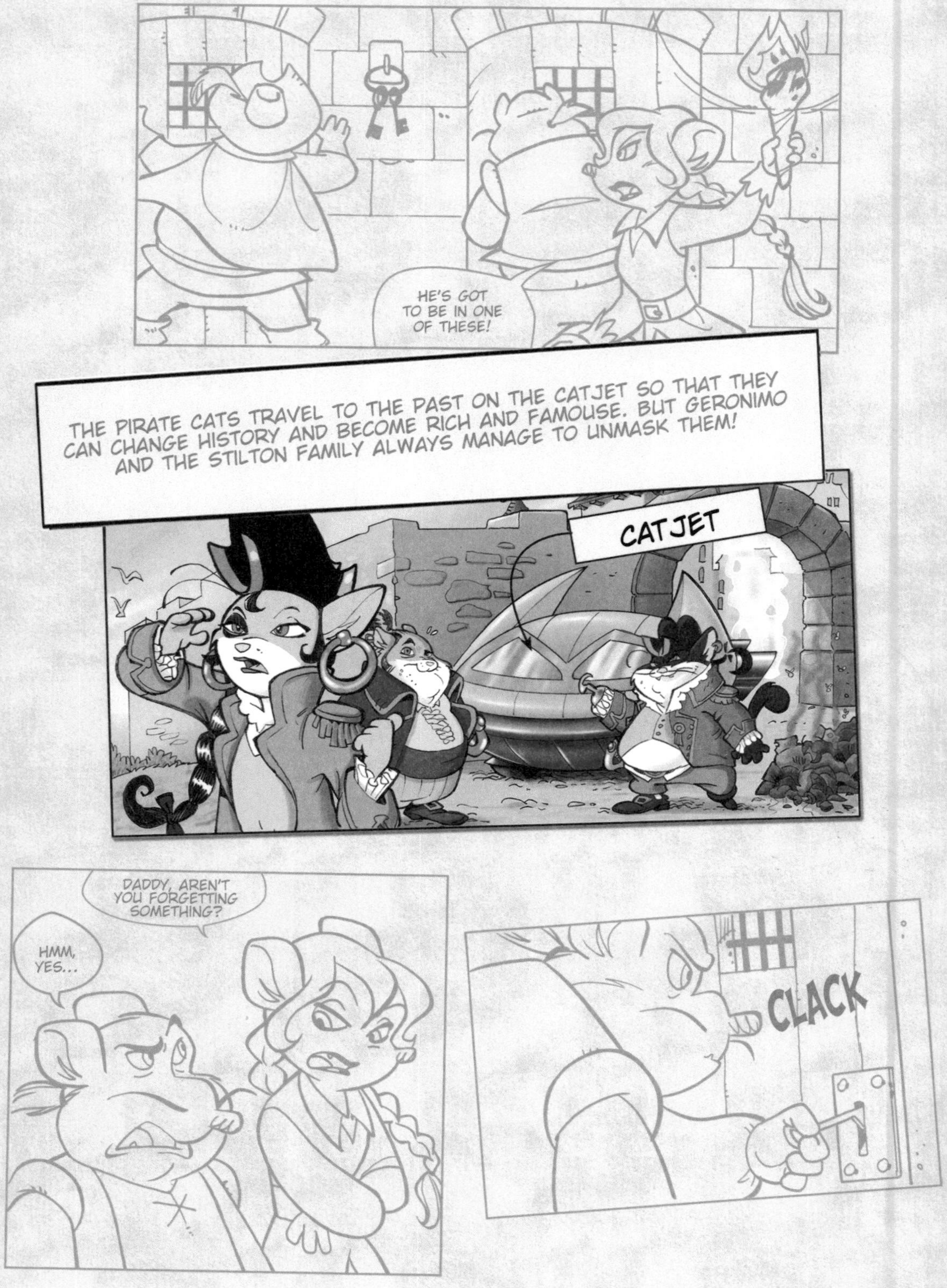
HE'S GOT TO BE IN ONE OF THESE!
THE PIRATE CATS TRAVEL TO THE PAST ON THE CATJET SO THAT THEY CAN CHANGE HISTORY AND BECOME RICH AND FAMOUSE. BUT GERONIMO AND THE STILTON FAMILY ALWAYS MANAGE TO UNMASK THEM!
CATJET
DADDY, AREN'T YOU FORGETTING SOMETHING?
HMM, YES...
CLACK